PRAISE FOR WRA

"Wrath James White is the premiere author of hardcore horror. Period."

> — EDWARD LEE, AUTHOR OF *THE BIG HEAD*

"Some of the ballsiest, most visceral fiction being written by anyone today."

> — THOMAS TESSIER, AUTHOR OF *WICKED THINGS*

"Wrath James White has more to say than many of his contemporaries, and says it more eloquently. "

> — POPPY Z. BRITE, AUTHOR OF *LOST SOULS* AND *EXQUISITE CORPSE*

"If Wrath doesn't make you cringe, then you must be riding in the wrong end of a hearse."

> — JACK KETCHUM, AUTHOR OF *THE GIRL NEXT DOOR* AND *RED*

THE ECSTASY OF AGONY

THE ECSTASY OF AGONY

WRATH JAMES WHITE

CL▲SH

To Mom

CONTENTS

Introduction by Edward Lee   xi

1. Beast Mode   1
2. 99 Cent   23
3. Krokodil Fights   41
4. First Person Shooter   55
5. Seven Years   75
6. The Ecstasy of Agony   87
7. Big Game Hunter   91
8. Unsolicited   105
9. Blood-Soaked Savior   117
10. Blue & Red   129
11. Punk Rock Revenge Porn   143
12. The Bliss Point   153
13. Horse   175
14. The Devil in The River   195
15. Screams in Bobby's Eyes   205
16. Eating With Momma   215
17. Big Brother   227

INTRODUCTION BY EDWARD LEE

In the realms of extreme horror fiction, there are writers, and then there's Wrath James White. Wrath plies the trade of hardcore horror with the expertise of an artisan; it's a hard business, and extreme horror begs criticism far more than other sub-genres. Indeed, every hardcore horror writer seems to have critical crosshairs on their backs. The chief complaint always seems to be a lack of discipline. "Oh, it's easy just to slop pornographic violence on the page!" Well, yes it is. One time a detractor said to me "Extreme horror is just a bunch of insecure guys circle-jerking each other, trying to gross each other out." Well, fuck you. Certainly there are bad examples in this field and, yes, some practitioners do demonstrate a showcase for haphazard writing and inane circumstances. Show me a genre that doesn't have its clunkers. However, Wrath James White, for as long as I've known him, has delivered some of the most sound and provocative extreme horror I've ever seen. What younger writers don't seem to understand is this: the secret to good extreme horror isn't the level of extremity in the fiction but the prosecraft. Using just the right words and arranging them with deliberation. That's what makes the fiction tick. That's what makes those outrageous over the top scenes so effective. You can have all the maggot-ejaculating zombies you want, but if it's not written well, it doesn't work. It's fuckin' boring and stupid. Wrath, on the other hand, is a technician with words, and the mechanics of his prose are the ingredients of his success. He's not just trying to gross us out, he's trying to make us think about what we really might do if faced with the scenarios that the characters find themselves neck-deep in.

This ass-kicking collection includes what has to be the most ghastly, the hardest core, and the most *wrong* prose poem ever written. Its images of close-up and personal body horror are rammed spiriferously (yes, that's a real word!) into the reader's brain where they will germinate without relent, turning your mind's eye into a kaleidoscope of 21st Century Hell. The concept is thus: addicts of the flesh-eating designer drug Krokodile are corralled into an arena and forced to fight to the death.

While they're literally *rotting*.

Amid the poem's frenetic energy and machine-gun bursts of appalling images, many readers might be inclined to ask: *Isn't the world horrible enough? Do we really need a poem like this?*

The astute answer, of course, is yes. We need all that and more so that we never forget that it's not all Facebook and Starbucks and Marvel heroes out there. It may seem like it. America has never been more selfish, narcissistic, and oblivious as it is today. That's why we need writers like Wrath, to remind us of our oblivion, to remind us that our society is a malicious meat-grinder that can't wait to haul our dumb asses into its choppers. We need poems like "Krokodile Fights" to remind us that shit like that–and worse–is really going on out there in the back alleys and unseen basements of this wincing, inexcusable, abominable and royally fucked up world we live in.

Oh, dear. That's not a very upbeat beginning, is it?

Oh, well.

Let me add that this collection divvies up, in between the stories, more horror poetry that all goes for the jugular. It's HARDCORE art for HARDCORE readers. I've never encountered horror poetry quite as powerful as this. And only Wrath is skilled enough to pull it off and makes us see what he's driving at.

Now let me touch on some of the stories. "Seven Years" you might think of as Wrath's gritty urban answer to Conrad's "The Secret Sharer." Wrath is known for out-right brilliant concepts (*The Resurrectionist* and *His Pain*, for example) and this story is a case in point. Every seven years, our bodies' cells replace themselves with new ones. Well...what happened to the old ones? Damn, why couldn't I have thought of that?

If ever there was such a thing as a zombie apocalypse, I'm pretty sure it would be grimly similar to "Beast Mode," where common everyday interactions don't change very much even when everyone outside wants to yank out your colon. Nihilism has never been this much fun!

"First Person Shooter" starts out with a couple of assholes stealing kids' Halloween candy and turns into a morality play that ends in, of all places, a video arcade. The plot device of someone getting physically pulled into a video game (a'la *Tron*, for instance) usually doesn't work for me. I just can't quite suspend my disbelief. But Wrath's take on this device is another matter altogether. There's something about his stylistic voice and his visual writing M.O. that makes this scenario chillingly, uncannily real–it's a smorgasbord of hardcore ghetto splatter. Our two protagonists (well, maybe that's not quite the right word) are slowly metamorphosed into a video game that makes *Grand Theft Auto* look like *Mr. Rogers' Neighborhood*. No one is safe in this game–trust me–not even pregnant women. Wrath's prowess with words not only convincingly puts the characters into the video game, but it puts YOU there too. Wear a raincoat! I'm kind of ashamed of myself for being so giddy while reading this.

Quality time between father and son goes WAY wrong in

"Big Game Hunter." If you want to talk about a dysfunctional family, ask Stanley about his dad, his Uncle Mickey, and the tube of Astro-glide. This delightful little piece answers the universal question: what makes a sexual serial killer? Well, here it is, folks! Fuck...

In "Unsolicited" we're treated to a threesome Wrath-James-White style. Holy shit, the things men do to impress women! And when Wrath wrote "Bliss Point," I'm certain that Billy Graham began lurching out of his grave. He might *still* be lurching, on his way to Wrath's house.

And there's plenty more. This work is all spot-on, dead-solid-perfect hardcore horror. It ain't easy writing an introduction for an author who NEEDS no introduction. Now more than ever, the face of our society is explicit, deranged, and abominable, and fiction that's the most relevant must always reflect some of that reality. Like *this* fiction. Wrath delivers that reality by the bucketload and dumps it on our heads. He's not gonna let us miss the big picture, because he's got some things to say. Important issues like child abuse, racism, political insanity, etc., all percolate between the lines here. This isn't Extreme Horror For Dummies—this material MEANS something, and we need to let Wrath fill us in.

Wrath James White has been doing this gig for at least twenty years, and I'm certain he'll be doing it for many more. In all that time, he hasn't missed a beat. Nowadays, there are a whole lot of horror writers out there, but the quality of this collection just goes to show you why Wrath stands at the very top of the heap.

Edward Lee
    Seminole, Florida
    July 14, 2022

Chapter One

BEAST MODE

Week 1. Day 1.

Went to the gym on the third floor. It took me a while to find it. In the four years I've lived in this building, the only time I'd ever set foot in the fitness center before today was the day the saleswoman walked me around to impress me with the condo's many wonderful amenities. There were six treadmills, six elliptical machines, three rowing machines, a pulley machine, a couple adjustable benches, a dumbbell rack with dumbbells ranging from 5lbs all the way up to 110lbs. It was pretty intimidating. Probably why I'd never used it before.

I pulled out my new bible, *BEAST MODE! 6 Week Body Transformation Workout*. This wasn't your normal body-building book. This was supposed to build functional, practical strength, and endurance. It was based on the workouts of Olympic gymnasts, sprinters, boxers, and wrestlers, written by a guy named Adonis Namor, who was a strength and conditioning coach for a couple of famous Mixed Martial Artists.

I turned to the first chapter, titled "Week 1," and read down the list of exercises. I groaned in genuine emotional pain when I spotted "Burpees" and "Mountain Climbers" on the list. Burpees reminded me of a sadistic gym teacher I had in junior high school who used to make us run a mile every day in the middle of the schoolyard, in the Las Vegas heat. I hated that bitch. Another likely reason I've avoided the gym for most of my life. Of course, there's also my visceral hatred of jocks, stemming from being a certified nerd throughout high school and college. Anyway, here's the complete list of exercises.

Warm-up with a 15-minute jog on the treadmill followed by:

15 burpees
   15 mountain climbers
   15 push-ups
   15 bench dips
   15 pull-ups
   30 squats (with light dumbbells or own body weight)
   15 crunches
   Side plank (30 seconds each side.)

Repeat 2 to 3 times.

I made it through once, then promptly vomited in the nearest trash can. But I forced myself to do one more set. Then I threw up again. This time I didn't make it to the trash can. Almost regurgitated a third time cleaning up the vomit from the gym floor. That's when I decided I needed to keep a journal of all of this. Have I mentioned that I am a smoker (was a smoker), a drinker, and that I am 30 pounds overweight? Big belly, big ass, skinny arms, man boobs. This is going to be hard. I haven't even begun the diet yet.

Low Carb, high fat, moderate protein. It's called the Primal Diet. I found it on an internet search of "best diets to get ripped quick." I liked the sound of it. There was irony to it. What it meant was that I could eat meat, dairy, and lots of vegetables. Only low-sugar fruits. No grains. No legumes. No sugar. No alcohol.

It said I should only eat fresh fruits and vegetables. Nothing processed. That was going to be hard under the circumstances. Luckily, I had lots of frozen vegetables that my ex-girlfriend had left in the freezer. Those would work.

Tonight's dinner: Broccoli and cheese and two burger patties. No bun.

Day 2.

Woke up this morning at 8 a.m. with a loud groan and a few popular words of profanity. My entire body was sore. I took as hot a shower as I could stand. The steaming water felt good on my aching muscles. Afterward, I threw on some boxer shorts and popped in a yoga DVD. After thirty minutes of poses and stretches, I actually did feel better. Maybe my ex-girlfriend wasn't such a kook after all. For breakfast, I made a two-egg omelet with onions, mushrooms, bell peppers, and aged cheddar, along with three pieces of beef bacon and a tall glass of milk. I read for a while. Wrote in my journal. Went out onto the balcony and looked out at the city, but I found it too depressing. Las Vegas was just one big festering pit of wasted dreams, wasted lives. Someone should have dropped a bomb on it long ago and put us all out of our misery. Fuck this town. I don't know why I stayed here for so long.

I decided to hit the gym early today. Made it through two sets of exercises without throwing up this time. For lunch, I had a can of sardines in olive oil and a salad. For dinner, I had a 16oz ribeye steak, two hard-boiled eggs, and half a bag of frozen green beans. I need to slow down on how much I'm eating. Don't want to run out of food. Working out just makes me ravenous.

Day 3.

Ran into the redhead from across the hall in the gym this morning. She looks amazing, but she talks too much. I don't watch the news because I don't want to hear about all the bad shit going on in the world. There's never anything positive on TV. The last thing I wanted was to have to hear a blow-by-blow of the latest atrocities when I'm trying to get my workout in. At least I got to stare at her tits. She has great tits. She was only wearing a sports bra when she ran on the treadmill beside me, and her D-cups were flopping all over the place. I was staring so hard I almost fell off the treadmill. Made it through three sets this time. I felt like the redhead was impressed, though she didn't really let on. I think she may have seen me staring at her tits. Now I feel like a jerk. I wonder if I should apologize.

Found some pork chops in the back of the freezer. They were shriveled and gray, completely freezer burned. No telling how long they'd been there. My ex-girlfriend was anti-pork. I had to have bought them before she and I started dating. That has to make them at least two years old. Probably older. But, beggars can't be choosy. Had them with the rest of the green beans. They were delicious. Well, kinda.

Day 4.

My body is so sore I want to scream. Did three sets again today. I want to say it's getting easier, that I'm getting stronger. But, I think it's all mental. I'm just getting used to the pain. This time I ran with the treadmill on an incline and I used ten-pound dumbbells when I did my squats. The redhead was there again. Her eyes were bloodshot. She'd obviously been crying. I asked her if she was okay, and she smiled and gave me a hug. Then she spent twenty minutes telling me about all the horrible shit going on in the world, and her life in particular. I listened even though I didn't really want to hear it.

I had a hard time falling asleep last night, despite being bored and exhausted. I kept having nightmares about being eaten alive. I could almost feel teeth ripping into my abdomen and tearing out my intestines. I woke up screaming. I did jumping jacks and burpees until I finally collapsed from exhaustion.

Day 5.

Only got three hours of sleep last night. I feel like hammered shit. Made another omelet for breakfast. Ate the last of the bacon. Starting to run out of eggs. Gonna have to borrow some from the neighbors. Maybe I'll see if the redhead has some. The workout was much easier today. Progress!

Day 6.

Rest day. Spent the day watching porn and reading comic books like I was back in high school. I needed it. Every time I tried to take a nap, I kept dreaming about getting torn apart. I'm just too sensitive.

Day 7.

Went over to borrow some eggs from the redhead. Finally worked up the nerve to ask her name. Cindy. First Cindy I've met since elementary school. I still think of it as a child's name. She said she used to be a stripper. I guess that fits. I traded her a couple of steaks for a carton of eggs. I invited her to dinner, but she said she wasn't in the mood for company. Fuck her. Did a different routine on the treadmill today. I started at 6 miles per hour then increased it every tenth of a mile until I got up to 8 miles per hour, then I'd start all over again. My lungs were burning so badly I wanted to stop after the first five minutes, but I made it all fifteen minutes. Tomorrow the workouts get harder.

Week 2. Day 8.

Twenty minute jog on the treadmill
    30 jumping jacks
    30 burpees
    30 mountain climbers
    20 pushups
    20 bench dips
    Set of 10 dumbbell bench presses with 25lb dumbbells
    20 pull-ups
    Set of 10 dumbbell curls with 15lb dumbbells
    Set of 10 shoulder presses with 15lb dumbbells
    Set of 50 squats with 20lb dumbbells
    Set of 10 lunges 20lb dumbbells
    Side planks (1 minute each side.)

Repeat 2 to 3 times.

I only made it through once. Natural, organic, all beef hotdogs and pickled asparagus tips for lunch. Hamburgers without a bun and salad again for dinner. Checked the scale. I've already lost 10lbs. I guess my body must be in shock going from fast food, beer, and apathy to exercise and zero carbs or sugar. Still have a long way to go.

Day 9.
Ran into Mr. Jenkins from the second floor. He didn't look so good. He always looks so angry. I can't say I blame him. Life sucks. I asked him if he had any canned vegetables. He said he hated vegetables. His wife filled the pantry with all kinds of canned food a few weeks before she passed, and he hadn't eaten any of it. Said he'd give me all of them for $100. I don't know what he planned to do with the money, but I paid him. My pantry is full now. There was a really bad smell coming from his apartment. I definitely heard someone moaning. I think I need to keep an eye on Mr. Jenkins. Only made it through one set of exercises again today. This shit is hard!
Had three eggs for breakfast. No bacon. Canned tuna and canned green beans for lunch. Cooked hot dogs and frozen peas and carrots for dinner.

Day 10.
Two full sets! Getting stronger! I read that fasting helps your body repair itself, so I didn't eat all day today. I'm going to be so fucking hungry in the morning!

Day 11.
More eggs for breakfast. Hard-boiled. Ate half a block of

cheese. About three-quarters of a pound, if I had to guess. Saw Cindy in the gym again this morning. She ran for a full two hours without stopping. I guess that explains that amazing body of hers. She had the incline on 6 percent and the speed at 7.5! I kept up with her (sort of) for the first ten minutes, then I said "Fuck that!" and put it back down to 6 mph and a 1 percent incline for the last ten minutes. I was exhausted when I got done, but I still managed to make it through two full sets of exercises again.

Ran into a kid running through the halls. No parent in sight. I asked him where his parents were, but he ran off. I hope he's okay.

Ate my last steak for dinner today. Starting to regret trading Cindy. It's just frozen hot dogs and hamburgers from here out. I do have one pack of frozen chicken fingers, but they're breaded. I could probably scrape all the breading off, though.

Day 12.

Three full sets! Who's the man? I'm the man! Saw Mr. Jenkins in the hall right after my workout. He looked even worse today. He tried to bite me, so I had to crush his skull with a 20lb dumbbell. Got brains and blood everywhere. I never realized the brain was so pale and squishy. It looked like a big nest of bloated larva floating in cherry Jello. Took me almost an hour to clean it all up and drag his body into the elevator, then down into the basement with the rest of them. So glad the power is still working. It would suck if I had to carry him all the way downstairs. Mr. Jenkins may not have liked canned vegetables, but whatever he was eating, he definitely wasn't missing any meals. Now I'm curious who that was upstairs moaning in his apartment? Mrs. Jenkins perhaps?

Ate canned tuna with lettuce and pickles for lunch, and corned beef hash and canned beets for dinner. I fucking hate beets.

Day 13.

Cindy invited me to her apartment for lunch. Steamed carrots and brussels sprouts with canned beef. It honestly wasn't as bad as it sounds and was still in line with my diet. She had rice with her meal, but I declined. Too many carbs, and rice also contains gluten, despite what the USDA says. Rice and corn farmers had their lobbyists make sure their crops didn't get added to the list of foods that contain gluten. So, even though corn has almost as much gluten as wheat, you can put both corn and rice in a product and still call it "gluten-free" and idiots buy it. I'm no idiot.

Cindy told me she was planning to run the 33.3 miles to Hoover Dam. That's where the roadblocks and barricades start. I asked her if she had any weapons. She didn't. I asked her what she planned to do if she got chased or surrounded. She said she'd just run faster. I didn't tell her how stupid I thought that plan was because my plan isn't a whole hell of a lot better. Besides, I really, really want to fuck Cindy. I know that sounds so sexist, but I haven't had sex in months. Not since my ex-girlfriend left. I wonder if she's still alive.

Three full sets again today. I can see my bicep and chest muscles developing. I wonder if Cindy notices.

Day 14.

Another rest day. Finally! Did yoga again. Getting a little more flexible. At least I can actually touch my toes now. That might also be because my gut isn't as big. Regular exercise and no more beer means no more beer belly. That's one good thing about all this. After a lifetime struggling with my weight, I finally have the proper motivation to get in shape.

Saw that kid again too. He was running through the halls with what looked like some kind of ninja sword. I think there was blood on it, but I can't be certain.

I decided to take a peek in Mr. Jenkins' apartment. He might just have guns in there. He seemed like the NRA type. Pretty sure he was a Republican. I also needed to deal with whatever was causing that smell. Everyone else in the building was too lazy or scared to do anything about it. Most of them never came out of their apartments anymore. That meant I had to do almost everything myself.

They had a tenant's meeting a few weeks ago, right after the building was locked down, to try to get some sort of cooperative effort going to share food and maintain the building. That day, I helped my neighbors clean up the building. That's when we decided to use the basement as a garbage dump and morgue. It was the only thing we could all agree upon. There was a lot of bitching and complaining, but no solutions. It was hard getting people to agree on anything during the best of times. You'd think a crisis like this would have brought out everyone's social survival instincts, made people more willing to work together for the common good, but it did the exact opposite. It made everyone more suspicious and self-centered. Myself included. I had never been much of a people person. My neighbors tried having a few more meetings, but attendance dwindled down to nothing. No one cared anymore. Everyone was just out for themselves.

I broke into Mr. Jenkins' apartment, had to kick down the door. There was a woman in his guest bedroom tied to the bed. Definitely not Mrs. Jenkins. This woman was too young and built almost as well as Cindy. Or had been before she'd begun to rot. One of her breasts had sunken in and deflated like a rotten grapefruit. I can only imagine what Mr. Jenkins had been doing with her. I bashed her skull in with a steam iron, then dragged her down to the basement too. I didn't bother cleaning up, though. Not my apartment.

I did find a handgun in Mr. Jenkins' place. I knew he was the type. It's a Sig Sauer .40 caliber semi-automatic with three full magazines. I guess I'm going to have to teach myself how to shoot. This might just make my plan a little more realistic. I also found a fifteen-pound sledgehammer in the basement when I was disposing of the body. That could definitely come in handy. I'll have to add it to my workout routine.

Mr. Jenkins still had a lot of other canned foods in his apartment. I found more Spam and corned beef than anyone had any right to have. There was also tuna fish and canned chicken. I found a big suitcase and filled it with as much food as it would hold. I figured I was entitled to it since I did clean up his mess. Well, I got rid of the body at least.

He had a bunch of frozen dinners too, but it was all full of carbs. Every last one contained a fuck-ton of cornstarch and corn syrup. The last thing I needed was to gain more weight. That would have completely fucked up my plans. I need to be increasing my strength, speed, and endurance, not chowing down on hot pockets and frozen pizzas. I left the frozen dinners for some other scavenger to find.

Week 3. Day 15.
New Workout.
30 minutes on the treadmill.
50 jumping jacks
50 burpees
50 mountain climbers
30 pushups
30 bench dips
Set of 10 dumbbell bench presses with 35lb dumbbells
20 pull-ups
Set of 10 dumbbell curls with 25lb dumbbells
Set of 10 shoulder presses with 25lb dumbbells
Set of 10 tricep extensions with 25lb dumbbells
Set of 50 squats with 25lb dumbbells
Set of 20 lunges with 25lb dumbbells

I found an old truck tire in the basement, hauled it into the service elevator and upstairs to the gym. I spent five minutes hitting the truck tire with the sledgehammer like they always show MMA fighters do during their workouts. Let me tell you, that shit is hard! I feel like I say that a lot. It's all hard, I guess. Either that or I'm just a pussy. I guess I need to "man up" if my plan is going to work. I need to get tougher, mentally as well as physically.

Back in my apartment, after my shower, I looked up MMA videos on the internet, trying to learn a few moves. I did my best to practice them and commit them to memory. It was challenging without a partner and without a teacher to tell me if I was actually doing the techniques correctly. I fell asleep watching Special Forces videos on shooting and hand-to-hand combat. Not sure how much, if anything, I actually learned. But at least I now had some idea how to use the gun I found in Mr. Jenkins' apartment.

Had hot dogs for lunch with a big hunk of cheese. Ate Spam and eggs for both breakfast and dinner along with half a pack of frozen peas and carrots.

Day 16.

Ran 40 minutes on the treadmill today. Not jogged. Ran! I thought I was going to die at first. The first twenty minutes were pure agony, but then my lungs just opened up and I could breathe again. I felt like I could run forever. I only stopped because my legs started getting sore. I'm thinking I might try to run to Hoover Damn with Cindy, if she'll wait for me. It's going to take me another ten or twelve weeks to get up to where I can run 33 miles, though. I don't think we have ten or twelve weeks. I guess it's time to up my mileage. Push myself a little harder. Down another four pounds. Less than four more weeks to go in my six-week body transformation! Hoping I can lose at least ten more pounds while also putting on another ten pounds of muscle. That should make running a lot easier.

Started another 24 hour fast. It does make me feel a lot more—I don't know—not to sound like a Scientologist or anything, but—clear.

Day 17.

Cindy ran for three hours today! At least that's what she said. She'd already been on the treadmill for over an hour when I walked into the gym. I pushed myself to run for an hour. Then I did three sets of my workout routine. I'm definitely getting a lot stronger.

I talked to Cindy about running to Hoover Dam with her. I told her I could help protect her. She said I'd just slow her down. Besides, I'd never be able to run 33.3 miles in a week. She was pretty sure she'd be ready to make the trip by next weekend. I told her I'd miss her, and she kissed me, right on the lips. I don't think I've ever been kissed by a woman that beautiful before. I almost came on myself.

I hit that tire with the sledgehammer for ten minutes straight with no breaks. My back is killing me!

Had scrambled eggs with canned mushrooms and artichoke hearts for breakfast. I've gotta say, it was pretty fucking delicious. Had tuna again for lunch. Made an egg salad for dinner.

Day 18.

Found out that kid has been hunting in the building, going from apartment to apartment, killing anything inside that wasn't human. Kid couldn't be more than ten years old. I asked him if he wanted to come to my apartment for something to eat, but he called me a pervert and ran off.

Ran for an hour on the treadmill again today, and I mean really ran! I had the treadmill set for eight-minute miles. Still not as fast as Cindy. She can run seven-minute miles for 18 or 20 miles. I'm still proud of myself. I've come a long way from the overweight, anti-social, couch potato I was. I watched a DVD of John Carpenter's *The Thing* before bedtime. Had nightmares all night. It might be a good idea to go back to Mr. Jenkins' apartment to see if he has any good DVDs. Horror movies are probably a bad idea.

Eggs for breakfast again. Tuna and canned spinach for lunch. Hamburger without the bun and canned green beans again for dinner.

Day 19.

Cindy knocked on my door this morning. She asked me if I'd seen that kid running through the halls with a samurai sword. I told her I was pretty sure it was a ninja sword and that he was going from apartment to apartment killing things.

"Things? Those things? Isn't he too young?"

I shrugged. I didn't think his age really mattered anymore. We were all probably going to die eventually anyway. What did it matter?

I invited Cindy to stay for breakfast. I made us both omelets with canned mushrooms, canned spinach, and American cheese. It would have tasted better with the aged cheddar, but I had already eaten all of it. While she ate, Cindy began talking about running to Hoover Dam again.

I asked her once more why I couldn't go with her. Once again, she told me I'd just slow her down. I told her I'd miss her. There was a little twitch in the corner of her lip, then a tear rolled down her cheek. She quickly wiped it away, then shoved more eggs in her mouth.

Day 20.

Had tuna fish and a hard-boiled egg for breakfast. I was on my way down to the gym when I saw that kid in the hallway again. Something is definitely wrong with him. He was hacking at some big fat guy with that sword of his. The guy was bloated and decaying, dripping rot and putrescence. His skin had begun to slip. The kid had already lopped off both the guy's legs and was still chopping at him with his sword as the fat guy crawled down the hallway. The boy stayed just out of reach of the big guy's snapping teeth, slinging blood and fetid meat onto the walls, floor, and ceiling as he continued hacking and slicing away at him.

The smell wafting from that guy was enough to gag a maggot. I couldn't understand how a kid could watch something like that, let alone participate in it. I could feel my own sanity slipping away just witnessing this carnage. I was holding on with everything I had, but I could feel my very soul screaming in horror. What the fuck was wrong with that kid? Too many violent video games perhaps?

Splashes of gore coated the boy from head to toe. His face was a dripping mask of blood and liquid rot, but his eyes were flat and dispassionate. He had dead eyes, oblivious to the horror around him. His face was completely expressionless as he chopped at the big guy's neck and shoulders with the sword. When the guy's head finally came loose, dangling from the bleeding ragged stump of his neck like some gruesome cat's toy, I wanted to say something to the kid, tell him he shouldn't be doing that. But I couldn't think of any reason why not except that I was the one who was probably going to have to clean it all up.

After spending a couple hours mopping and scrubbing the hallways, I went to the gym and ran for more than an hour, until I almost fell off the treadmill. I skipped lunch and dinner. Just wasn't in the mood to eat.

Day 21.

Cindy knocked on my door again this morning. I was so tired. I barely slept last night. I kept thinking about that kid hacking that guy to pieces like he was cutting beef. All the blood and bits of rotten fat and muscle tissue that had littered the walls and floor. God, that shit was fucking horrible!

I was still thinking about it when she walked in wearing nothing but a bathrobe. She was completely naked underneath! She laid down on my couch, opened her robe, and spread her legs, revealing a perfectly shaved pussy. It was one of those moments you read about in the forum section of men's magazines. The type of shit I'd always been certain never really happened to anyone. But there I was, staring at the type of body I normally only saw on the cover of fitness magazines, legs spread, arms outstretched, gesturing for me to join her.

I went to lay down on top of her, fumbling with my belt, but she took me by the back of the head and guided my face down between those smooth, freshly-shaved thighs. She must have just showered because she smelled like lavender and vanilla. I licked her pussy until she came. The entire time she kept telling me how much she needed this, then she thanked me and left. Never touched me. I popped in a porno and jacked off three times, then ate a couple eggs and went down to the gym.

One hour on the treadmill, three sets of exercises, ten minutes swinging the sledgehammer, followed by some yoga. I wasn't really feeling any of my DVDs. Luckily, the internet is still up and running. I watched sitcoms and action movies until I fell asleep.

Day 22.

Decided to practice with the gun. Went out on the balcony and shot off a few rounds. Didn't hit much. My apartment is too high up. But I did get the hang of working the safety, using the sites, and not flinching in anticipation of the recoil. I don't want to use up all the bullets, so I guess that's the best I can do.

Did three sets of exercises and ran for an hour. Then I had

some canned chicken, canned spinach, and boiled some frozen asparagus.

Day 23.

Rest day. Ate some eggs and cheese. Did some yoga. Tried to sleep. Dreamt about the boy chopping the fuck out of that fat guy every goddamn time I closed my eyes. Decided to say fuck a rest day and went down to the gym for a run. Ran six miles. Tired as fuck now. Still can't sleep. Ate two cans of tuna and a can of fucking beets. Ran out of green beans, and I'm trying to ration the spinach. God, I fucking hate beets!

Day 24.

Saw Cindy in the gym this morning. First time I saw her since she came to my apartment the other day. She smiled and waved, then put on her headphones and jumped on the treadmill. Why are the beautiful ones always such assholes?

I ran six miles again today. I have to say, I'm pretty impressed with myself. I've lost more than twenty pounds in less than a month and I feel strong as a fucking ox! I think this might work. Ate a can of potted meat. That's what it was called. Potted meat. Never heard of it before. It was just salty chunks of beef. Dog food for humans. Had the last of the frozen peas and carrots before remembering that peas are fucking legumes! So, not exactly in keeping with my Primal diet. Fuck it. One day of carbs won't hurt. Not like I'm eating ice cream and pizza.

Day 25.

Cindy knocked on my door again this morning. She was wearing the same robe. Naked underneath again. I started to protest. To stand up for myself. But she surprised me. She dropped the robe, walked right past me into my bedroom. I seriously wish I had cleaned my bedroom. It was covered in dirty laundry and cum-crusted towels. Cindy didn't seem to mind. She laid down on my dirty, sweaty, semen-stained sheets, spread her legs and said those two words every man dreams of hearing: "Fuck me." I didn't have to be asked twice.

Neither of us went to the gym today. We stayed in my apartment, fucking, eating, and talking. Cindy said she was leaving tomorrow. She was ready to try to make it to Hoover Dam. I asked her why she had to run the whole way? She could just run to the nearest car and drive to Hoover Dam. She shot that idea down, pointing out that the streets were jam-packed with vehicles and that she didn't know how to hot-wire a car anyway. To take her own car, she'd have to open the garage, which meant unlocking the entire building and putting everyone inside at risk, and then there would still be the problem of the clogged streets.

"What about a bike or a motorcycle?"

Same problem with the motorcycle. No keys, and she couldn't hot-wire one. She said she'd thought about the bike, but the streets were littered with glass and debris. Falling off a bike and hurting herself would make her even more vulnerable. Running was her best bet. That's when I told her my idea to fight my way out. That's why I've been doing so much strength training. I figured I could just fight my way all the way to Hoover Dam, or at least until I found a spot where the roads were clear and I could borrow a car. She asked me if I was serious, then told me it was the dumbest plan she'd ever heard. We laughed about it, then had sex again.

I scraped the breading off the chicken fingers and cooked them for us along with my last can of spinach. I wanted to beg her not to go, but I understood. Staying locked up in this building, waiting to be rescued, wasn't an option. Plus, she'd been following the news, and she was pretty sure the government was planning to nuke the place in the next few days. The only thing saving them so far was a Congress that couldn't wipe its own ass without arguing about it. But soon, they would give the order, and Las Vegas would be a big mushroom cloud.

"I don't think you're going to have the time to get in the kind of shape you want to get in," Cindy said.

I told her about the gun and the two-and-a-half magazines of ammo. My plan was to use the sledgehammer to crush skulls until my arms got tired. Then I'd switch to a small hatchet I'd had since I was a young scout. Then, when I was too tired to fight anymore, I'd use the gun. By then, hopefully, I'd be somewhere safe. Another building, a car, somewhere, and I'd just keep repeating that process all the way to Hoover Dam. She nodded at me and smiled. It was the kind of smile you gave someone to boost their confidence before a contest you didn't think they had any chance of winning. The kind of smile normally followed with platitudes like: "It doesn't matter if you win or lose but how you play the game." Only, it did matter this time. Losing meant death or worse.

"I think you're already pretty badass, though. Maybe you can make it."

Maybe. That's what kept me up all night. Maybe. While Cindy slept, snuggled up against me, I decided I wasn't going to let her go without me. I was going to protect her. I would make sure she made it. It occurred to me that, before all of this, a girl like her would have looked at a guy like me and thought, "Not if he was the last man on earth." Cindy may have thought the same thing about me that first day in the gym. Now, we were in bed together and I was considering risking my life for her. Funny how quickly shit can change. As far as Cindy was concerned, I was the last man on earth.

Day 26.

Cindy left without telling me. I woke up to her screams. I ran to the balcony, and I could see her down in the street, getting chased by dozens of rotting corpses. They were pouring out of the buildings on both sides of the street; out of stalled cars, SUVs, trucks, and buses; out of the casinos, bars, restaurants, and gaudy tourist trap souvenir shops. A massive wave of rotting humanity, flowing through the streets like sewage, heading in her direction. Hundreds of them. There was no way she was going to make it. I grabbed a pair of cargo shorts I'd selected weeks ago to wear when I made my own bid for freedom, the hatchet, the sledgehammer, and the gun. Shoving the magazines into my pockets, I ran down eight flights of stairs, unlocked the front door, and raced up the block.

I heard footsteps behind me and turned to see the kid with the ninja sword running just a few strides behind. I nodded to him, and he nodded back as we raced into the fray. Cindy had been cornered against a bus when we caught up to her. I yelled and started swinging the sledgehammer. Skulls cracked and ruptured like week-old Jack-o'-lanterns as iron met bone. I saw Cindy go down, watched her stomach get ripped open, her organs torn out in fistfuls and consumed. Heard the sound of skin and muscle tissue ripping and tearing, bone and tendon breaking, ghoulish slurping and chewing mixed with her ear-piercing cries of agony. Her pink flesh stretched like taffy as they tore her apart. She was beyond help. We locked eyes for a moment, and a look of utter shock, disbelief, and disappointment crossed her face. I couldn't tell if she was disappointed in herself for not being able to outrun them or in me for not rescuing her. Then her pupils dilated and fixed in place as her life fled.

I heard the boy cry out from behind me. He was getting overwhelmed. The dead had surrounded him, and his sword arm was obviously getting tired. He was about to suffer the same fate as Cindy.

I fought my way to him, and together, we ran back to the condo. We were both covered in blood and rot when we pulled down the security gates and locked the doors behind us. We collapsed on the floor of the lobby, breathing hard, trying to catch our breath.

"Did you get bit or scratched or anything?"

The boy shook his head. His eyes were wide, and he was breathing hard, but he was smiling. He nodded toward me, too exhausted and out of breath to ask the question.

"No. None of them touched me. Not a scratch."

I thought about Cindy. All that training. All that work, and it hadn't helped her. She didn't even make it a mile. But my training had come in handy. I had killed more than a dozen of those things, and I managed to save the boy. Fucking Beast Mode for real! Who'd have ever thought a guy like me could go from zero to hero in only a month? Almost a hero, that is. I hadn't been able to save poor Cindy. I remember the look of pain and horror on her face, how her eyes had pleaded with me to save her while she was being ripped apart. That look will plague me for the rest of my life, however long that is.

I closed my eyes and let out a sob. Tears began to flow. Then I heard a sound that made me think I may have just gone insane. Laughter.

I opened my eyes, and the boy was sitting up, decorated in blood and bits of decayed flesh, laughing like he'd just had the time of his life. Like he was watching some hilarious cartoon or had just ridden the world's greatest roller coaster.

"That was pretty awesome! When do you think we'll be ready to try again?" he asked.

Crazy fucking kid.

"About two weeks and four days," I said. "Give or take."

Let's just hope Congress continues to hold their gridlock. Maybe long enough for me to get the boy in shape too. Can't have his sword hand getting tired again. This is going to be hard.

Chapter Two

99 CENT

"What would you do for ninety-nine cents?" I asked.

I was being an asshole. That's what you do when you're out wandering Sixth Street on a Friday night with your friends. They're trying to cheer you up because your girlfriend just dumped you for some other guy after you'd told them all that you were planning to propose to her. You get all your loud, obnoxious, single, and really-ought-to-be-single, misogynistic, jerk male friends together. You go down to Sixth Street. You get drunk. You hit on every girl you see, make fun of those less fortunate than you, maybe start a fight, and end the evening throwing up in your best friend's car or passing out or getting arrested. Unless you are lucky enough to get laid, which isn't likely. I was well on my way to door number one.

My stomach sloshed, roiling with ten beers and half a dozen shots of Jägermeister, threatening to revolt at any minute. The sidewalk was undulating, some huge serpentine creature traveling unseen just beneath the surface of the pavement, beneath the heels of my shoes, throwing me off balance. Several times, I had to lean on Johnny or Eddie to keep from falling flat on my face, which made them laugh. Seeing someone at the brink of alcohol poisoning always struck them as funny.

I don't know how or why we began teasing the homeless, but Mikey started it. We passed a group of homeless runaways carrying backpacks and wearing hiking boots, like they were just going camping for the weekend rather than making a horrible lifestyle decision that would gravely impact their futures. One of them, a blonde girl in her late teens or early twenties with her hair twisted into unwashed dreadlocks, was carrying a sign that said "Will Work For Food."

"Yeah, but will you fuck for food?" Mikey asked, then doubled over with laughter.

"You don't have enough money to get in my panties, jerk!"

"Well, how about a blowjob for fifty bucks?" Mikey asked, his mood and expression suddenly serious.

I could see her considering it. The two young couples with her perked up, looking at her expectantly, already calculating how much weed, acid, and extras they could buy with fifty bucks plus whatever else they'd accumulated from begging all day.

"Fuck you!" she said, and everyone let out a collective sigh of disappointment. Her friends were even more disappointed about losing the fifty than Mickey was about not getting his dick sucked by a homeless chick.

We all laughed.

"You're crazy, Mikey!" I said, then wobbled again as the sidewalk slithered beneath me, stumbling into him and almost taking Mikey to the pavement with me.

"Sorry, dude!"

"You're fucking toasted, dude! You gonna be all right?"

"I'm fine. I'm fine," I said, waving off his concerns.

Eddie and Johnny were staring down the homeless chick's

boyfriends, who were going from being upset about losing the fifty to demanding ten dollars for insulting their friend.

"Kiss my ass, fool! We ain't givin' ya'll shit!" Eddie shouted. Eddie was big, just shy of six-five. He had an athletic build that made him look huge when he was shirtless or in a tank top or tight-fitting t-shirt, but tall and skinny if he was in long sleeves. Tonight, he was in long sleeves and a gray cardigan, looking every bit the data analyst he was rather than the hardened gangster he was trying to sound like. But he was black, so even when he wore his ridiculous red bowtie (which he had thankfully spared us all from this night) he could usually intimidate white people whose only exposure to black America came in the form of hip-hop videos and crime statistics. These kids weren't buying his act, though, and a back-and-forth shouting match was beginning to heat up.

"I should call the cops and tell them you offered me money to fuck you!" The young blonde said.

"Yeah! We should get all you bastards locked up," said one of her brave male protectors with a big red beard and what looked like a curly red afro framing a moon-shaped, almost luminescent, white face exploding with freckles.

In the middle of all this, I spotted the homeless woman on the next corner holding a sign that said simply "$1." She was older than the blonde with the dreadlocks. Probably old enough to be her mother. But she looked too young to be as down and out as she apparently was. Not that there's an age limit upon misfortune, but there's a type, and she didn't fit it. She was somewhere in her early- to mid-thirties and looked like she'd been on the streets a long time. She had that thousand-yard stare you get when you've seen and done much too much. The look soldiers and prostitutes get. Too old to be a teenage runaway. Too young to be a bag lady. That left crackhead, meth fiend, or one of those unfortunate thousands that get let out of mental institutions when they run out of space or funding.

"You'd better get the fuck out of my face, motherfucker!"

"Then pay my girl here the ten dollars for offending her honor."

"Honor? She's a fucking homeless skank!"

"I ain't payin' that ugly bitch shit!"

"Oh, but I wasn't ugly when you were offering me money to fuck you."

"I never said I'd fuck you. I said suck my dick. You ain't got to be pretty to give a blowjob. Every girl looks pretty with my dick in her mouth."

"Fuck you!"

"Fuck that bitch!"

Their voices were just background noise, like I was underwater and they were all somewhere outside. Even their images seemed wavy and distorted. The only person I could see clearly was the homeless woman across the street.

She had long, limp, oily brown hair, a profusion of long-healed acne scars, piercing blue-gray eyes that reminded me of a wolf or some bird of prey. She was skinny but looked strong. Her triceps were a perfect horseshoe, and her biceps were knotted into a little, hard tennis ball-sized muscles. She had large breasts that had sagged prematurely. Probably because she wasn't wearing a bra beneath her "Hook 'em Horns!" t-shirt and probably hadn't in years. She was missing a tooth in the front, but the remaining ones appeared healthy and relatively clean. She had a bruise on her cheek and the eye above it was bloodshot like she'd recently taken a punch. She looked like the type of woman who would have taken Mikey's offer of a blowjob for fifty bucks.

I kept staring at her sign. Perhaps it was Mikey's solicitation of the blonde homeless chick coloring my perception, but the sign she held gave me the impression of a price tag. One dollar. This was how much she thought of herself. That was her worth in her own estimation. And I was so drunk, so self-absorbed by my own petty misery, being dumped by a girl I did nothing but argue with when she wasn't completely ignoring me, that I wanted to depreciate her even more.

"What would you do for ninety-nine cents?" I asked her.

She turned her cold predator-gray eyes toward me, and held me in her steady gaze. In a firm, sober voice, she replied, "I'd kill for you."

It caught me off guard. That had certainly not been the response I'd been anticipating. I laughed, and the force of my own laughter almost knocked me off my feet. A tidal wave rolled through my stomach, silencing my laughter as I fought to keep from throwing up. I was still giggling a bit when I replied to the old woman's bizarre offer.

"Okay, then how about killing my ex-girlfriend?"

"No problem," she said, holding out a hand that was stained brown with Lord-knows-what.

I reached into my pocket and withdrew some change, counting out three quarters, two dimes, and exactly four pennies. Ninety-nine cents, and not a penny more.

"Done," she said, pushing the money into some hidden pocket beneath her shirt, then leaning back and closing her eyes.

I laughed. "Yeah, sure."

The woman raised her eyelids and stared into my eyes.

"I said, it's done. You want her dead? She will be dead."

I held up my hands in mock surrender, giggling, swaying as if there was a strong breeze pushing me about, though the air was still, and trying my best not to fall on my ass.

"Okay, okay. I'm sure you're an expert assassin, cleverly disguised as a filthy, diseased, old homeless bag," I said, laughing and shaking my head, wishing my friends were over here listening to this craziness instead of across the street harassing those homeless kids and probably about to get their asses kicked.

"I told you. I got it. Go home and sleep it off. In the morning, the job will be done."

She closed her eyes again, seeming to nod off in a narcotic stupor. I stood there a while longer, staring at her, trying to decide if there was any possible way she was for real and feeling like I might have just done something unexpectedly terrible. A wave of guilt came crashing down on me like a tsunami, enhanced by alcohol and a liberal arts education steeped in political correctness that made such things as hiring an indigent vagrant to kill your ex-girlfriend shameful. I was about to tell the woman to forget about it when the absurdity of it hit me and I began to laugh. The entire situation was ridiculous. There was no way in hell this burnt-out homeless chick was going to go to my ex-girlfriend's apartment and murder her for ninety-nine cents. I was drunk, this woman was crazy, and that was as far as it went. I shook my head and laughed again, feeling like an idiot for worrying.

Over the next two or three hours, Johnny, Eddie, Mikey, and I drank more beer, hit on more women, and somehow all made it back home to our apartments alive and without DUIs. The next morning, I was awakened by the doorbell, followed by a heavy fist pounding on the door like they were trying to take it off the hinges.

I staggered out of bed and stumbled into my bedroom wall. I fell against it hard enough to leave a dent in the sheetrock. Had the wall not been so close to the bed, I'm certain I would have fallen straight to the floor. My head felt like it was under attack by little gremlins with jackhammers and pickaxes. The room blurred and did a little pirouette that made my stomach flutter. I took a few steps, arms held out at my sides to balance myself on the imaginary tightrope that stretched from my bedroom to the front door. The doorbell rang again, followed by someone pounding on the door even louder than before. I imagined my old, cheap, wooden apartment door cracking and splintering, and my skull doing the same. I closed my eyes and swallowed, trying to block out the noise and the pain. Hangovers suck.

"Hold on! I'm coming, damnit!" I yelled as I staggered my way through the apartment. "Who the hell is it?"

I was certain it would be one of my idiot friends, come to continue last night's party. I fully expected to see Johnny or

Eddie or both of them standing outside my door, holding a bong in one hand and a six-pack in the other, grinning like monkeys with a fistful of shit. The last thing I was expecting to see were police officers.

"APD, Mr. Seever. Open up. We need to ask you a few questions."

A cold, damp, cloud of dread enveloped me. I peered through the peephole at the two cops, and my scrotum shrank up tight against me. I tried to remember everything I'd done last night. My imagination conjured up half a dozen horrible offenses a bunch of drunk, socially-awkward geeks may have possibly committed that would merit police attention. Then I remembered the homeless woman and her promise to murder Amy for me.

One of the cops was a burly black guy in uniform, the other, a tall, slender Asian man dressed in a suit straight off the rack from JC Penny's. A detective. A homicide detective. I was certain of it. Just as I was certain, the moment I opened the door and asked the detective how I could help him, he was about to tell me ...

"Your ex-girlfriend, Amy Weinthrop, was found dead in her apartment this morning. Murdered."

Impossible.

The humidity in the apartment increased, becoming a sauna. I found it hard to breathe, hard to see. Everything became hazy, like summer heat waves rising off the asphalt. It was hard to think, hard to concentrate. The air was too dense and warm to swallow. I choked it down with effort. My skin was hot and sticky. Perspiration dripped down my face and the sides of my body.

"What? What did you say?"

"I'm Detective Woo. This is officer Tanner. We're here because your ex-girlfriend was murdered last night."

The blunt, pitiless way he broke the news to me made it clear that he believed me to be a suspect.

"Where were you between the hours of midnight and two a.m. last night, Mr. Seever?"

"I ... uh ... I was drunk. On Sixth Street. With some friends. Amy left me. She ... she left me for another guy, and my friends were trying to cheer me up. Help me forget about her."

"And they will corroborate this?"

"What? Yeah. Of course."

"What are your friends' names?"

"Eddie, Mikey, and Johnny."

"Last names?"

"Oh, yeah. Ummm? Eddie Dominic, Mikey Lassiter, and Johnny Brown."

"We are going to need to know their addresses and phone numbers."

"Yeah, yeah, of course. How, how did she–um–how did she die? I mean, how was she killed?"

"Some sick piece of shit tore her to pieces. I'm going to have to ask you to come down to the station with me."

Again, no tact, no attempt to break the news gently. He didn't even try to spare me the more gruesome details. Just the raw facts laid bare, hurled in my face with every intent to wound me. I was aware that both the detective and the other officer were watching me, gauging my reaction to the news. I reacted all over their shiny black shoes.

"Awww! Goddamnit!"

"I'm sorry, detective. Sorry! I just–Urrrrrrlgh!"

I threw up again. This time I rushed past the two officers, hanging over the side of the second-floor railing and hurling into the parking lot below. Luckily, no one happened to walk by at the time to receive a non-consensual Roman shower.

After giving the cops the contact information for my three drinking buddies, I allowed them to search my house. They were thorough, checking places it would have never occurred to me to hide anything, in my freezer, couch cushions, AC vents, my bookshelves. They even scooped up the meal I'd just regurgitated and spooned it into little baggies. I wasn't sure what they were looking for, but I was pretty sure they didn't find anything. They asked me if they could see my emails and texts. I told them they couldn't have my phone or my computer, but I downloaded copies of everything onto a thumb drive and gave it to them. The two cops were hovering over me the entire time, making certain I wasn't trying to hide or delete anything incriminating. Finally, I agreed to go down to the station. It was evident from their demeanor that it wasn't really my choice.

The next three and a half hours I spent at the station, chatting with Detective Woo like we were old friends catching up on each other's lives. I was expecting the "good cop/ bad cop" routine I'd always seen on television cop dramas, but all the detective did was talk to me. He asked me about my childhood, my job, my hobbies. We talked about art and politics, past girlfriends, my crazy friends and all the stupid shit we did when we hung out. Detective Woo told me all about his family, his old college frat boy days. Turned out we belonged to the same fraternity. We even laughed together about an ex-girlfriend of his who always tried to speak to him in Chinese phrases she'd learned online even though he was Korean and only spoke English. The entire time they kept bringing me coffee. It wasn't until the third hour that the detective asked me the first question about Amy.

"So, why did you and Amy break up? Was it because of your friends? She didn't like you hanging out getting drunk? My wife is always nagging me about drinking with the other cops on the weekends. But, you know, a man needs time to relax and unwind, right?"

"No, it wasn't anything like that. We just didn't agree on anything. Politics, movies, how I comb my hair, the clothes I wear, the way I kiss. To tell the truth, I don't know why I didn't leave her first. Except she was so damn beautiful, and the sex was amazing. I know that's shallow, but it's the truth."

As we talked and drank coffee, a technician from the

Crime Scene Unit came in and took an impression of my teeth. That's when Detective Woo showed me the photos of Amy. He was right, she had been torn apart. She'd been disemboweled and nearly decapitated. Her woman parts, breast, vagina, and most of her uterus, had been removed with some sort of jagged instrument, ripped away like in chunks.

"Her killer did most of this with his teeth," the detective said, which explained why they wanted the teeth impressions.

I felt my stomach bile rise and choked it down with a grimace.

About forty minutes later, they let me go.

"Well, your alibi checks out. But don't leave town. We might have some follow-up questions for you."

Two officers drove me back to my apartment building and dropped me off. I was still in the same sweaty clothes I'd worn the night before. When they left, I sat alone in my apartment, trying to come to terms with what had happened. A homeless woman murdered Amy, tore her to pieces, because I put a dollar in her cup. Correction. Not a dollar. I'd been too cheap for that. Ninety-nine cents. I had to find the woman.

And what? Call the cops? Make her confess somehow? Kill her? I didn't know.

I changed clothes quickly, grabbing a t-shirt from my laundry basket, a pair of jeans from the floor, and some socks from my drawer, hastily assembling them into some semblance of acceptable attire, then left my apartment, sober but still in desperate need of more coffee and clarity. I just needed time to think. There was a sensible explanation for all of this, something I just wasn't seeing. I was certain of it. Long ago, I had come to the realization that life was just like a complex computer code. When something went wrong, it was inevitably due to one small mistake. All that was necessary was to go back through all those lines of code and find that one small error—the missing quote, the backwards slash, the incorrect numerical sequence—that was causing the entire program to malfunction. Fix the error, and everything would run smoothly. That's all I needed to do, find the error and fix it. That brought me once again to the homeless woman. She was the key to figuring out why Amy was dead.

I shambled from my apartment and through the parking lot in a lurching, stumbling, fugue-state, not seeing my surroundings but operating on instinct and memory as I made my way to my little 10-year-old Honda Element. Luckily, it was in the same place I always left it. My mind was too preoccupied with the puzzle of Amy's death, which was looking a lot less puzzling by the moment. The more I thought about it, the more convinced I became that it was exactly what it appeared to be. I had hired a psychotic derelict to murder my ex-girlfriend, and she had succeeded. But the why of it continued to elude me. Ninety-nine cents. That's what didn't make sense. That and how she had known Amy's name and address. It felt almost ... supernatural. But I didn't believe in such things outside of role-playing games and sword and sorcery movies. Yet, I couldn't think of any other explanation, except coincidence. Ghosts and demons somehow sounded more plausible to me at that moment than Amy just happening to get eviscerated by a psychopath the same night I paid a crazy woman to end her.

Perhaps the woman was some sort of demon, and by hiring her, I had sold my soul. Maybe there are hell-hounds coming to collect my immortal spirit right at this moment.

It sounded insane. But last night, the idea of a homeless woman killing Amy for less than the price of a candy bar sounded ridiculous too. And I had no idea how any of this supernatural shit was supposed to work. Eddie would know. He was into all of that Aleister Crowley, H.P. Lovecraft stuff. He read horror novels and comic books about angels and devils, zombies and demons taking over the earth, and he watched horror movies fanatically. Eddie's favorite RPG games all had plots built around biblical and Pagan mythology. He even played video games with biblical themes like Knights of Hell and Heroes In Purgatory. I didn't know if he was really a believer, but he was a fan of the mythology, and that made him the closest thing I had to an expert.

It wasn't until I reached into my pocket for my cell phone and realized it was already in my hand that I became aware I was already in my car, pulling onto the freeway on-ramp with no memory of ever opening my car door, starting the vehicle, or driving out of the parking lot. I dialed Eddie's number.

"Yo, dude. I heard about Amy. Some detective called me this morning asking if you were with me last night when she got killed. I'm so sorry, man. I know you really loved her and shit. I mean, she dumped you, and then this shit happens? That's some fucked up shit. You think that guy she's dating now did it?"

In all of my theories about supernatural homeless women/demon assassins, the most plausible scenario, that Amy'd simply hooked up with the wrong guy and he'd turned out to be a serial killer or something, had never even occurred to me. Maybe this was all just one big coincidence?

"I ... I don't know, Eddie. I mean, I never met the guy. But that has to be it, right? I mean, who else would do something like this?"

"Unless, it was just some random killer. You know, wrong place. Wrong time. Maybe it's a serial killer that's been stalking her for weeks and, now that you aren't with her every minute of every day, he thought this was the perfect opportunity to strike."

I felt that now familiar pall of guilt and remorse, which had lifted for a moment when Eddie suggested it had been her new boyfriend who'd murdered Amy and not a deal I'd made with the devil, descend once more with the inevitability of nightfall.

"So, you're saying if I had been with her last night instead of out drinking with you guys, Amy would still be alive?"

"Maybe, but that wasn't your choice, right? She left you, remember?"

"Yeah, I remember."

"Look, this wasn't your fault, dude. Don't take this shit all on yourself."

I nodded, knowing Eddie couldn't see the gesture through the phone. But that's the only acknowledgment I had the energy for.

"Eddie?"

"Hmm?"

"What do you know about demons? I mean like demonic possession, making pacts with Satan, that type of thing?"

"Fuck are you talking about, dude? Why you asking me this shit?"

And so, I told him. Everything.

"So, you think Amy's dead because you gave some homeless chick ninety-nine cents? Man, you're just crazy with grief. There wasn't no homeless chick even there last night. I mean, just that one teenage skank and her friends."

"You guys were busy fighting with those kids. You didn't see her. She was right across the street from where y'all were standing."

"There was nobody there, man," Eddie said with a sigh.

"I saw her, dude! I talked to her. She was in her early thirties, looked like she'd been through hell, like she'd been in a fight recently. But it was more than that. She had this faraway, haunted look, like my brother had when he came back from Afghanistan. And she was all beaten up, like she'd just gotten her ass kicked, but something about the way she held herself, you knew whoever she was fighting, the other guy got the worst of it. You know what I mean? She had scabs all over her face, a black eye, a missing tooth, and hard lines like she'd been out in the sun too long. I mean, she looked terrible, but she still had this arrogance about her. Like she was better than me even though she was the one out there begging. And she had this little cardboard sign that just said, one dollar."

"I'm telling you, man. You walked across the street and were standing there, looking like you were going to throw up. I walked over and got you myself. I had to hold you up just so you could walk back across the street. There was nobody there with you. You didn't sell your soul to kill Amy, dude. That's just your grief, sixteen or seventeen beers, and like six shots of Jägermeister talking."

He was probably right, but I needed to see for myself. I hung up the phone just as I approached the first downtown exit. That's when I saw her wild red eyes and bruised, battle-scarred face in the rearview mirror.

"So, who's next?"

I screamed and jerked the wheel, almost swerving the car over the embankment on the side of the off-ramp. My first instinct had been to stomp on the brakes, which would have definitely resulted in my little Honda getting rear-ended at sixty-five miles an hour. Luckily, I managed to keep the car steady. My heart was now thundering in my chest, and I could feel a warm wetness spreading between my legs.

"What the fuck are you doing in my car?"

She looked exactly the same as she had last night on Sixth Street, only there were scratch marks on her face and neck now, deep gouges through which stringy red muscle tissue was visible. A smear of red stained her mouth and cheeks like she'd been face-first in a cherry pie. She looked like a disheveled clown painted in blood.

"I'm here for the next target. I took care of that whore for you. Who's next?"

I closed my eyes and shook my head, but the ghastly creature remained, grinning at me from the back seat, wearing that same smug expression.

"You actually k-killed her? I was just joking! I was drunk and pissed-off. I didn't think you'd actually do it!"

She frowned at me, then smacked me in the back of the head.

"Of course I killed that little cunt. That's what you paid me to do, ain't it?"

"Paid you? No. No. No, I was just kidding! It was just a fucking joke! I mean ... it was just ninety-nine cents! I didn't mean it. I didn't mean for you to–oh my God. Oh my God." I rubbed the back of my head. This woman was crazy, a murderer, and I was alone with her in my car. I could not imagine many scenarios where this would end well for me. I briefly considered diving out of the car.

"Yes, you did. You were hoping I would. You wanted that little cunt dead, and now she is. So, who's next?"

"No one! That's it! This ends right here!"

Her bony fingers encircled my throat. Long fingernails black with fungus, some broken or raggedly bitten off, dug into my skin as she squeezed my windpipe shut. The pain was instant, like I'd swallowed burning charcoal. My lungs struggled for oxygen. I gagged and coughed. Spots danced in front of my eyes and leaked tears down my cheeks while I struggled with one hand to keep the car on the road and with the other to pull her gnarled talons from my throat.

"Is that what you think? You think this shit is over? You and me, we got a relationship now."

Her laughter was a robust cackle that filled the car like it was coming through the sound system. She let me go and I sucked in a breath that burned its way down. I began to cough again. More tears came flooding out now in a pathetic deluge of self-pity. I sobbed openly, terrified for my life.

"But ... we had a deal! You were supposed to kill Amy and that's it!"

The homeless woman smiled, a self-satisfied grin that tore across her blood-smeared mouth like an open wound.

"Oh, but didn't you just say you ain't really want her to die?"

"Okay! I wanted her dead. But that was it. You said– "

"I said I would kill for you, and I will, every day, for the rest of your life. My price was ninety-nine cents, the price you bartered for, and you paid it. Now I am your own personal assassin. Just point me at a target and I will go to work."

"I don't want you to kill anyone else! I just want it to end!"

The woman leaned forward again and seized me by the hair, jerking my head back and whispering in my ear in a raspy growl that raised goosebumps up and down my spine.

"It doesn't end until there's no one left for me to kill, and you'd better hope that day doesn't come ... for your sake."

Tears and snot had formed a trail down my face. I had no more shame.

"Pleeeeease! Please just go away!" I wept.

"Then give me the next name!"

And so I did.

She told me to pull over on Second Street and let her out. I tried pleading with her one last time not to do this, but she gave me a slap that busted my lip, bloodied my nose, and sent the mixture of blood, snot, and tears splattering across my dashboard. Then she stalked off into Zilker Park. She paused and whispered back over her shoulder, a whisper that sounded like a shout to my ears.

"I'll be back tomorrow for the next name."

No, no, no, no, Noooo! This can't be happening. This just can't be fucking happening!

I punched the dashboard a few times, then just sat there in the car, sobbing like an infant, but not one of those tears was for Amy, or for my asshole boss who would be dead by the morning. Right then and there, I decided the next name I gave her would be her own. I didn't know what her name was. I had never bothered to ask, but I would just tell her to kill herself, and she would have to either obey or break whatever contract she believed she had with me. Then it would be over. I would be free, and my life would go back to normal. At least I hoped it would be that simple. It had to be. I had no other plan.

I turned the car around, not knowing where I was headed. In minutes, I was pulling into a parking lot under the bridge just off Sixth Street. From where I was parked, I could see the spot where I'd first met the homeless woman the night before. There were three cops, a van with "Medical Examiner" on the side, and four or five other guys, one taking photos, one bagging evidence, and several others that just appeared to be waiting, milling around the area. The scene was roped off with yellow police caution tape, and a small crowd was beginning to form on the other side of it.

Two guys in blue jumpsuits with "M.E." written on the back were leaning against the dark blue coroner's van, their cell-phones in hand, tapping their feet and repeatedly rolling their eyes, sighing, and checking watches they weren't actually wearing. Apparently, whatever the cops were doing, they weren't doing it fast enough.

Who did that crazy bitch kill now? She couldn't have killed my boss already?

But I was certain that whatever had drawn the coroner's van to that spot had something to do with "my own personal assassin." I felt sick. My legs shook as I stepped out of my little Honda. There was a stain on the front of my pants from where the homeless woman scared the piss out of me. As much as I wanted to get back into my car and drive far away, another city, another state, I had to walk across that street to see what had happened, and I was sure it would be something horrible.

I gently pushed my way through the crowd, which had doubled in size in the minute and a half it had taken me to cross the street. When I reached the tape, I spotted the same detective who had come to my door less than an hour ago. Detective Woo. He spotted me too.

"Well, this is a coincidence, isn't it? Two deaths this morning, and this is the second time I see you. Was she an ex-girlfriend of yours too?"

"Who? Who is it?"

"I was hoping you could tell me," the detective said as he walked over to the body.

It was a windy day, and the sheet covering the corpse blew aside, giving me a clear view before one of the officers tucked it back into place. It was the homeless woman. Someone had dragged her off the sidewalk, behind some bushes, and torn her apart. Her sign was still lying beside her, her throat flayed open to the bone, her torso split from asshole to appetite and completely hollowed out. Her internal organs were everywhere, decorating the shrubs, the mulch, the flowers, the grass, dripping red meat strewn about her haphazardly like a kid rushing to open a present and tossing wrapping paper in all directions. Most of the blood had already soaked into the soil and mulch. Everything was painted a brownish red. I stared at her face. She appeared to be smiling at me. So much for me telling her to kill herself. She had already taken that card off the table. Whatever she was now, whatever had just been in my car, I realized with a shudder, ghost, demon, worse, it was beyond death.

The detective was watching my face, trying to read me. He saw the expression of horror on my face when I recognized the homeless woman. His eyes narrowed, brow furrowed, and he raised one eyebrow

"So, any ideas who I'm looking at?"

I continued to stare down at the corpse, searching for the error, that one mistake that, once fixed, would set everything right again, and finding nothing. I had set in motion an unbreakable infinite loop of murder.

"We can do this here or I can slap you in cuffs and we can do this back down at the station," the detective said. He was just doing his job. If it wasn't him harassing me it would have been some other cop. It didn't matter. It had to be someone. And I now had the next name.

Chapter Three

KROKODIL FIGHTS

Shambling scarecrows
Scraps of clothing hanging from our bones
in careless tatters
Scraps of flesh hanging from our bones
in painful, ghastly ruin
living zombies
if this nightmare existence
could be called living
by anyone
except morbid lunatics
and delusional junkies

We were undead
but not living
Existing
but not living
Rotting alive
Soon-to-be corpses
lumbering awkwardly
from one high to the next

on aching bones
loosely draped in meat
Nightmare creatures
damned by our addiction
created
of
our addiction

His blackened meat
fetid
rancid
putrefying
muscle
fat
skin
sloughed off
in chunks
like pork left too long
in a pressure cooker
on a barbecue
blackening
loosening
falling off the bone

I saw a floater once
at Pier 39
Floated up during lunch hour
between the sightseeing cruises
and the tourists
snapping photos
of corpulent sea lions

It had been dead
for days
floating in the polluted water

amid waste and fast-food wrappers
in the Frisco Bay
Bloated
purple and black
meat and skin sliding off
slippage
they called it
like the flesh
on Michael's arm
slipping off
leaving holes
revealing
pearlescent bone
pink sinew
Still
he
kept
sticking
the needle
in

He passed it
to me
Krokodil
Desomorphine
Synthetic heroin
codeine
caustic soda
gasoline
hydrochloric acid
iodine
and red phosphorus
from a box
of Lucky Strike matches
Krokodil

Like being eaten alive
by carnivorous
prehistoric reptiles
But slower
slower
slowly
consumed

We looked like zombies
Alive
but not living
We were undead
But not for long
Not for long

I could see my humerus
Peeking through
the gaping wound

I could see my femur
in another wound
My pelvis
in another
My ribcage
through the newest one

I knew a guy
who shot Krokodil
into his neck
until all the muscle
rotted away
His head fell
He
kept
sticking
the needle

in
Almost decapitated himself
He's dead now
Rotted away
Floated away
Head
Fell
Away

It's been two weeks
since they found me
Promised me
Promised us
all the Krokodil we could inject
in whatever flesh was left
to take a needle
hundreds of dollars
enough to buy the real shit
The shit
that doesn't
make
you
rot
Not your flesh
just your soul
Hundreds of dollars
or death
and death
eventually
A slow
rotting
death
Like being eaten alive
By carnivorous
prehistoric reptiles
But slower

slower
slowly
consumed

We just had to fight
They just wanted
to watch the junkies fight
Watch the undead
the not dead
not alive
kill each other
Watch the rotting flesh puppets
marionettes of diseased meat
flail at one another
for another hit
of caustic opioids
Another opportunity
to kill ourselves
slower
slowly

I couldn't whore anymore
not even for necrophiliacs
I was too
far
gone
like walking carrion
Too bad the tricks
weren't more open-minded
I had more orifices now
Plenty of holes to fuck
Enough slick
supporting
boy pussy
for a dozen hungry cocks
But, no one

would fuck me now
Not even
the necrophiliacs
Not even
If the unctuous putrescence
leaking from my wounds
made them slick as wet pussy
more slippery than Astroglide
No one
would fuck me now
too bad

I imagined eager perverts
thrusting brutal cocks
into my gangrenous orifices
A gang-bang of
blood
semen
pus
and fetid meat

No love
for the man with a dozen assholes
So
instead
we fight

I started shooting in my good thigh
Injecting that ravenous reptile
into the femoral artery
I was worried
It would start rotting
like the other one
More black bleeding holes
I wouldn't have a leg to stand on
Can't stand

Can't fight
Can't fight
Die

It was the only vein
I could find
except
the one
down there
Not that far gone
yet
Not ready to lose my dick
yet
limp and useless as it was

They brought us to the cage
naked
They wanted to see
the horror
our addiction had made of us
They wanted to see
the holes

Someone rang a bell
Someone pointed a spotlight
Someone aimed the camera
A referee told us the rules
No rules
Except
fight hard
Fight or die

I threw a punch
It connected with teeth
He had no cheek left
on that side

just teeth
smiling like an idiot
like a pervert
like a lunatic
a psychotic villain

His teeth flew
Three of them
bounced and rolled
across the canvas
Two of them
lodged in my knuckles

He spat out a chunk
of something
shiny wet
Bloody and pink

He threw a kick
That landed
On my exposed ribs
Where skin, fat, and muscle
should have been

My ribs broke
splintered
Pierced my lungs
He kicked again
Before I could react
then rained down punches
with that lunatic
gap-toothed
Jack-o-lantern
pervert smile

The pain

stabbing
wrenching
churning
agony
made me vomit
something shiny wet
bloody and pink
then something else
purple and red
More
More
A tidal wave of
organs
blood
and whatever the fuck I'd eaten

I wanted to get high
I didn't want to fight anymore
Didn't want this rotting
grinning
punching thing
on top of me

Wanted to sail away
on a euphoric wave
of synthetic heroin
I wanted to escape the pain
escape the horror
escape the leering faces
of the audience
of the lunatic
pervert
Jack-o-lantern
killing me

I pulled him closer

hugged his broken body
put my mouth
to the loose
putrefying
gangrenous
flesh
of his throat
felt the pulse
of his heartbeat
in his carotid artery
embedded my dull teeth
pulled and tugged
Until my mouth filled
with wet metallic
meat and blood

My opponent
dug a thumb
into
my eye
it squished and squirmed
blue-white light flashed
white-hot agony
My own screams
pierced my ears
like hypodermic needles

I needed a fix
needed to get high
fly away from this pain
I released my grip on his throat
took skin
muscle
veins
spurting arteries
chewed and spit

something shiny wet
bloody and pink

I bent over
regurgitated again
An elbow crashed against my skull
blue-white light flashed
the room tilted
floated
flipped
turned gray
then black

The tug of jagged teeth
broken shards of teeth
biting at my face
biting at my chest
at the wound
where I used to inject
where my pectoral muscle
used to be
where my heart
beat wildly
Like being eaten alive
By carnivorous
prehistoric reptiles
But slower
slower
slowly
consumed
down the throat of the Krokodil
What the Krokodil had made us
Nightmare creatures
damned by our addiction
created
of

our addiction
murdered
by
my addiction
by the Krokodil

The audience cheered.

Chapter Four

FIRST PERSON SHOOTER

Marshall was sixteen now. That meant he was well past the age of trick-or-treating. He was almost six feet tall, though he was skinny as a scarecrow. His sweatshirt hung off his gangly limbs like it was still draped on a hanger in his closet. His friend Steve was the precise opposite, short and athletic with hard little muscles bulging everywhere on his 5'5" frame. Marshall imagined Mike Tyson probably looked similar at that age. Whereas Marshall's sweatshirt was too big for him, Steve's black thermal shirt was deliberately too tight, so each muscle was accentuated.

Instead of trick-or-treating, he and Steve went out bag snatching, just like their parents had done when they were their age and their parents before them. Only this wasn't the seventies or eighties anymore. This was the kinder, gentler, touchy, feely age of timeouts and participation trophies. Little kids didn't walk by themselves anymore. Their parents followed them door to door, hovering over them like vultures over roadkill. Even in the hood, tolerance for the normal mischievous kid-type crimes was gone. If you egged someone's house on mischief night, there was a high probability of either catching a case or a bullet.

Back when Marshall's dad was a teenager, the most he'd have to worry about was someone sending their big brother to find him and kick his ass. Now, Marshall had only managed to snatch two bags before someone called the police and the night lit up with blue and red flashing lights, making the Halloween masks and decorations look even more garish and frightening. Like a Mardi Gras in hell.

The last bag the two of them snatched was from a kid no older than nine or ten with a perfectly round, shoulder-to-shoulder afro, wearing a Superman costume and tan Timberland work boots. He was tall for his age, so he didn't have too many years of trick-or-treating left. Marshall felt a little bad ruining what may have been the kid's last one. But the first thing you learned growing up in G-town was the game was hard and never fair. People were divided into predators and prey, criminals and marks, victims and victimizers. In G-town, calling someone a "player" was redundant. Everyone was in the game, whether they realized it or not. From the grandmother just trying to cash her social security check and get home without getting rolled by some crackhead, to the single mother juggling three jobs while trying to keep track of her four kids from three different absentee fathers, to the teenaged killers selling drugs and doing drive-bys on rival drug dealers in an effort to control a few taxpayer-owned city blocks, all the way down to the young kids just trying to make it home from school without getting hit by crossfire or recruited into a gang. There was no sitting on the sidelines, no idle spectators.

Marshall snuck up behind the kid in the Superman costume and snatched the bag out of his hands. The boy tried to hold on, but the effort yanked him off his feet, dragging him down face-first to the cold asphalt. He looked up with eyes wide in shock, and then anger. There was a lump on his forehead now with an abrasion where his head had scraped the blacktop. There was dirt in his afro, and it had lost some of its shape. Its perfect spherical geometry had lost its symmetry, smashed down in the front and pushed back away from his bruised forehead. A trickle of blood dribbled down his face, and the kid casually wiped it away before it dripped into his eyes, gritting his teeth against the pain. Kids who made it past elementary school age in G-town didn't cry anymore. They learned the futility of it early on and either grew depressed, aloof, or hard, calloused, and angry. There were a few stubborn optimists, but they were rare. Those were the ones who could see a way out of the hood. They were good in school or athletics or had some other talent they were counting on to lift them out of poverty. Few of them actually made it. This kid was the calloused and angry type, the type that would grow up to carry a gun and spread his pain like a virus through the rest of the community. Marshall felt a momentary pang of guilt for contributing to this cycle of woe, but then his own street-hardened heart remembered all the times he'd been rolled for candy, money, shoes, jewelry, or his pride, beaten up just because someone else was having a hard day and beating the shit out of someone weaker was the only way they knew to make them feel better about themselves.

It's nothing personal, little homey. It's just your turn.

The kid looked at the bag of candy in Marshall's hands, then back up at the bigger kid's grinning face.

"Give me back my candy!"

Marshall laughed and shook his head.

"You mean my candy."

"Give me my damn candy!" he yelled more forcefully and hopped to his feet with both hands raised into fists. He bit his bottom lip and drew his right arm back to throw a punch.

Steve stepped forward and pushed the kid down.

"This little thug was about to swing on you, yo," Steve marveled.

The kid screamed like he had been mortally wounded as we ran off with his candy. It wasn't seeing all of that sugar, fructose, and cornstarch he'd acquired in an hour of door to door begging run laughing down the street, it was the blow to his pride. It was realizing his place on the food chain. Steve and Marshall had just shown the kid that he was prey, and his whole perspective on the world had been altered in that moment. The streets had become more threatening and dangerous for him.

"Hey, stop messing with those kids. I'm callin' the cops!"

It was old Ms. Nichols, the stereotypical nosey old spinster who was always peeping out her windows, watching what everyone was doing, and getting in everyone's business. If you played your music too loud, smoked weed, or drank beer before you were 21, she was the one who called the police on you or told your parents.

"Ay yo, we'd better get off the street before we get locked up or shot or something. I think that old lady called the police. Kid ain't hardly have shit in his bag anyway. This Halloween sucks," Steve said.

"Let's go hang out at that pizza joint on the Ave. You know, the one with all the arcade games. Crazy Cal's place?"

"Cool. But we'd better stick to the alleys. Cops is killin' brothers nowadays, if you ain't heard. I ain't tryin' to get shot over a bunch of Twizzlers, Now n' Laters, and Starbursts."

"You got Starbursts? I'll trade you for some Tootsie Rolls?" Marshall said, peering down into the bag he'd just snatched from the kid in the Superman costume. It was filled with chocolate, but Marshall wasn't a huge fan of chocolate. It was okay, but he could only eat so much of it before it made his stomach hurt.

"Naw, fuck that. I hate them things."

The screech of tires turning the corner and the explosion of flashing lights illuminating the darkened street got them moving. Steve ducked into the nearest alley. Marshall followed at a full sprint. He wasn't sure the cops had seen them, but he wasn't taking any chances. Getting caught would mean an ass-whoopin' from the cops and then another one from his mom once she bailed him out of jail. And that was if the cops didn't just execute his black ass in the street. Steve was right. Cops were killin' brothers nowadays. It was like that old NWA song, police in G-town thought they had the authority to kill a minority.

It took them almost half an hour to make it to the pizza place, running through alleys and hopping fences. Marshall and Steve knew the neighborhood backwards and forwards. They knew which yard to run through to take them from one street to the next the fastest. They knew to avoid Mr. Hightower's yard because of the two rottweilers he had that he'd turned vicious through abuse, and to steer clear of the alley that connected Tulpehocken Street to Duval Street where thugs from Eastside traded drugs for sex with hollow-eyed crackwhores. They knew the alley that would take them from Green Street to McCallum was a shooting gallery filled with desperate junkies, stumbling around like the walking dead and nodding off in dark corners. They used to avoid that one too, when they were younger. It wasn't exactly beneath a junkie's dignity to rob a little kid. But now that they were older and bigger, Marshall and Steve had no fear of the withered ghosts of humanity that rotted their bodies and brains in that alley. It was just another shortcut, no different than the rest.

When they reached G-town Ave, they climbed a fire escape and took to the rooftops, hopping from one building to the next for an entire block. They did it more out of habit than necessity. It was one of the paths they had taken since they were little, when they used to make this run for fun rather than to evade the police. There used to be a cinnamon-complexioned woman in her twenties they'd once caught masturbating with her bedroom window open. The next night the two of them had come back with a bunch of their friends and a pair of binoculars, watching from the roof of the building next door, hoping to catch her in the act again, but her window had been shut and the curtains drawn. Marshall had continued coming back every day for two weeks before he was finally rewarded. One night he caught the woman and her boyfriend fucking with the windows closed but the shades wide open. He'd even taken a cellphone video of it to show his friends. It was still on his phone. She didn't live there anymore, but Marshall still got excited when he passed that rooftop, as if she might come back unexpectedly and give them another show.

"Yo, Marshall. You remember that fine-ass redbone that used to live in that apartment?"

"Yeah, I remember."

"You still got that video?"

"Yup."

"We should watch it again later."

Marshall shrugged.

"There's better things on the internet."

"Yeah, but this is better because it's real."

When they finally made it to the arcade, they were lucky to find the place still open, though it was nearly empty. Most people were at Halloween parties, out trick-or-treating with their kids, or snuggled up with their lovers watching horror movies on Netflix. They were the only two fools out playing video games. Marshall and Steve were both out of breath when they stumbled through the doors with their bags of stolen candy.

"Damn. That was a lot of work to avoid getting caught stealing some fucking Halloween candy."

"Man, cops ain't playin' these days. I know a kid, you know Fat Sid from Eastside?"

"Yeah, ain't he in jail?"

I nodded.

"That fool got locked up doin' the same thing we just did. He snatched a couple bags on Halloween, and he got hit with aggravated robbery charges."

"For stealin' candy?"

"Yup, one count for each bag he snatched that night."

"Damn. That's fucked up."

"That's that new zero tolerance shit. I told you, these cops ain't playin' these days."

"That's seriously fucked up."

"Well, to be real, though, those kids who got their bags snatched after trick-o- treatin' all night probably think that shit's pretty fucked up too, though."

"Yeah, that shit happened to me two Halloweens in a row when I was little. Both times I made my mom get me a new bag and we went back to every house we'd gone to before and got more candy. I didn't sit around cryin' about that shit or get nobody arrested like these soft-ass motherfuckers now."

Marshall shrugged.

"Yeah, well shit was different then. My mom talks about how she used to be able to smoke weed with the neighbors on her front porch. Now the cops would be all over your ass if you did that shit. They say that makes the neighborhood safer, but all I see it doin' is making people hate the cops even more. Just like that stop and frisk bullshit."

"What's up, young bloods," Cal called out from behind the counter. "Crazy Cal" was in his fifties, a veteran of one of those wars nobody remembers anymore like Grenada or El Salvador, and he was crazy as fuck. All he ever talked about was pussy.

"Why ain't you two out getting' some of that young pussy? Man, when I was your age, I stayed balls deep in some pussy. Youth is wasted on y'all young motherfuckers."

There was something creepy about Cal, beyond his obsession with fucking. Something about his pointy nose, narrow, shifty, Asian-looking eyes, and too-thin lips that made his wide mouth look like a gash slashed into his face.

What black man had lips that thin?

It didn't help that he called everyone "blood" like he was stuck in the seventies. Cal also seemed to have an obsession with dead things.

A dried chicken foot hung from an inch of silver chain dangling from his left ear. He wore a ring with a scorpion encased in amber on his right hand and had an amulet on his chest with a tarantula suspended in glass. He dressed in black jeans, a black leather blazer, and a black bowler hat like Run-DMC, except he wore pointy, black, alligator-skin cowboy boots instead of shell-top Adidas.

There were rumors that Cal was a satanist or something, but nobody really believed that bullshit. There were much worse things to worry about in G-town than Satan. The devil would get his bitch-ass blown away just trying to cross Chelten Ave. At least that's what most people thought. Others were convinced G-town was another chamber of hell and that Lucifer himself ran everything from the street gangs to the liquor stores to the churches, right down to that shitty fried chicken place on the corner of G-town and Chelten Avenue. Marshall was pretty certain the salon that did his sister's hair weave was run by demons. Her skin was much too dark for bright red hair extensions, but they'd somehow convinced her she looked good in them. There had to be something evil about that.

The arcade, if Cal's low-budget Chucky Cheese could be called that, had about a dozen video games that changed every couple of months. It still had an original Asteroids and an old Centipede game that looked like they'd been there since Marshall's mom used to come there when she was a kid thirty years ago. An old B.I.G. song blasted through the sound system with enough bass to make Marshall's chest vibrate. It wasn't an unpleasant feeling. They both nodded their heads and sang along as they walked through the place checking out the newest games while Cal followed them with his creepy slanted eyes.

"Hey, young bloods. Check out this first-person shooter game I just picked up. It's dope as fuck. The graphics are fuckin' sick!"

It was one of those new games you played while wearing

virtual reality goggles. The game was called "Active Shooter" and it had two nine-millimeter Glocks that looked real and were supposed to kick like a real gun. There were other weapons as well, hanging on the sides of the machine. Two shotguns, an AK-47, and even a machete. But it was the game itself that was the most eye-catching. The CGI was insanely detailed, and the kills were brutal. Disembowelings, beheadings, dismemberment, all shown in graphic detail.

"Yo, you just walk around shooting and killing everybody you see? It's like some Columbine type shit," Steve said.

"You can kill cops, kids, fuckin' nuns. You can even rape bitches in this thing! I mean full on porno style!" Cal said with unnerving enthusiasm.

"Yo, I can't even believe they would make a game like this. You'd think people would be protesting about it."

Cal nodded proudly.

"And there's knives and axes and shit you can use too. This shit is fuckin' ill, blood."

"You got any cash? It's five dollars for two players," Steve asked, reaching an empty hand out toward Marshall.

"Damn, fool! Why you always broke?"

"Your momma got expensive tastes. You got the money or not?"

"Yeah, fool. I got it. Wit' yo' broke ass!"

"Then what you waitin' for? Let's play this motherfucker!"

They sat down in the chairs, put on the virtual reality helmets, and chose their first weapons. Marshall chose the shotgun, and Steve, predictably, went for the AK. Steve slid a five dollar bill into the machine and pressed the button for two players. The machine gave them a choice of locations. One was downtown. One was a shopping mall. There was a police station, a hospital, and a high school that looked a lot like G-town high. The last one, the one Matshall chose, was just called "The Hood".

"Bruh, is this really what they think the ghetto looks like? It's straight out of New Jack City."

"More like Menace II Society. Shit, it almost looks like our neighborhood."

"That don't look a damn thing like G-town. We ain't got all those junkies, crackheads, and crackwhores just stumbling around everywhere like that. And there ain't gangbangers on every damn corner. That does kinda look like your grandma's house right there, though."

"Why you always got to be talkin' shit about people's moms and grandmoms?"

"I ain't talkin' shit. That does look like your grandma's house."

"Bitch, fuck you!"

Steve laughed hard, holding his sides and rolling around in his seat, until Marshall began laughing as well.

"You ain't funny."

"Then why you laughin'?"

"Cause you so stupid."

The "hood" in the video game was a run-down block filled with dilapidated buildings, many of which appeared ready to collapse into rubble. The streets were dark and bustling with activity as drugs, sex, and guns were sold and people were robbed and assaulted at regular intervals. Marshall thought it was depressing that this was how the world saw them. They certainly didn't live in paradise, but Marshall didn't think he knew any place this bad. The neighborhood in this game was like something from a ghetto horror flick. Like what G-town would look like if it was in a Tim Burton movie. Or maybe one of Lucio Fulci's crazy-ass horror films. In that way, it seemed like the perfect game for them to play on Halloween.

"Have fun, youngbloods," Cal said, sliding out of view with a crooked toothy grin on his creepy, thin-lipped mouth.

"All right, let's kill some shit!"

Marshall picked up the shotgun and jacked a round into the chambers. He had never held a real shotgun before, but its weight felt right. Just how he would have imagined a loaded shotgun would feel. Hip-hop music began to play. The first person he saw was an old derelict wearing dirty pink and white mittens, the kind a young girl would wear. The old bum clutched a wrinkled brown paper bag, crushed into the shape of the liquor bottle it concealed, to his torn and soiled army jacket. His gray sweatpants hung low, revealing a pair of jeans underneath that were two sizes too big with a thick leather belt around his waist holding them up.

"Hey, doesn't that look like– "

Before Marshall could finish that thought, Steve unloaded on the old drunk with the AK. The man screamed as bullets tore through his body. He looked like a paper mâché' doll at the end of a water hose. The bag in his hands exploded as did the wino's skull, coming apart like a 3-D puzzle.

Just as Cal said, cops rushed onto the screen, only to be mowed down by gunfire from Steve's AK. Marshall took aim at a couple gangbangers in saggy jeans, blowing the legs off one and putting a hole in the back of another. The guy he shot in the back dragged himself along the sidewalk, his legs trailing uselessly behind him. His face grimaced and strained, sweat raced down his forehead, and a look of genuine terror filled his eyes before Steve finished him off with a hail of 9mm bullets.

"This is fun as hell!" Steve shouted.

Another group of police officers rushed onto the screen, and Steve dropped his AK and picked up an ax. Marshall grabbed the Glock and put half a dozen bullets in the chest of a redheaded officer who pleaded for his life before Steve cleaved his skull in two with the ax.

Marshall saw a guy who resembled Fat Sid, one of the local thugs who liked to rob and bully all the younger kids. Sid had stolen his bike once when Marshall was only eight years old. He'd just gotten that bike for Christmas when Fat Sid knocked him off of it and took off on it. Marshall picked up a switchblade and rushed over to the guy, stabbing him in the belly and ripping it upwards, opening his jiggly corpulent abdomen up from waist to sternum. A steaming pile of organs and intestines spilled at the Fat Sid lookalike's feet. Marshall had never gotten that bike back, but killing this virtual Sid felt like closure somehow.

Beside him, Steve had changed weapons again. He shot a pregnant woman with his shotgun, blowing a hole in her bloated tummy. A fetus spilled out onto the concrete as the woman fell to her knees and tumbled backwards, whacking her skull against the concrete steps of the porch behind her with a wet, sticky, "Smack!" The woman had been pushing a stroller, and Marshall took aim at that, emptying the rest of the fifteen-round magazine into it.

Another policeman rushed over to the dying pregnant woman, and Steve blasted him with the shotgun too. The cop's chest exploded with red, and he dropped hard on the canvas with a loud, blood-curdling scream. Marshall dropped the Glock and picked up the machete, lost in the seductive violence of the game, consumed by bloodlust, the feeling of power, and the sheer adrenaline-fueled fun, the entertainment of killing. He walked up to the nearest house, where the pregnant woman still lay sprawled on the concrete, her entrails spilling out of the two fist-sized holes in her belly. The fetus that had been inside her seconds ago lay in chunky red pieces beside her. A few feet away, the infant she'd been pushing in the carriage that was now tipped over on its side and riddled with bullet holes lay dead on the sidewalk. Where its face should have been, the skull had been caved in by gunfire like a deflated football. Through the virtual goggles, Marshall looked down at the woman. She was gasping for air. A rattling wheeze came from her throat and blood poured from her stomach like rainwater off a roof. An expression of abject horror scarred her face, and tears wept from her eyes as she reached out for the vandalized corpse of her dead child. Marshall felt chills race up his spine.

"This looks so real."

"It's fucking awesome!" Steve replied with macabre glee.

Marshall opened the front door and entered the house. There were women inside, teenaged girls, women in their twenties and thirties, and even one or two in their forties, all in various stages of undress. There were a few guys there as well, rolling off the women they'd been openly copulating with on the warped wood floors and cracked tile, reaching for their pants or their guns, or both. It was a whorehouse.

"Jackpot!" Steve called out beside him, and Marshall felt his stomach lurch. This was about to get really bad. He swung his machete down onto the wrist of the nearest guy as he reached for the Uzi beside him. He hacked the guy's hand off, then swung the machete at his throat, lodging it in deep. The guy fell over with the machete still embedded in his neck, spraying gallons of blood like an open fire hydrant on a hot summer day. Marshall picked up the Uzi. Steve had an ax and was chopping up two other guys and a couple crackwhores in the corner across the room. With each swing of his ax, blood splattered the walls; meat and limbs fell in a grotesque jumble at Steve's feet as he hacked his way through a forest of writhing arms and legs. Screams, prayers, and curses echoed loudly all around. The room was quickly soaked in blood that ran down the walls, coated the floors an inch deep, and dripped from the ceiling. It was only then that Marshall realized that Steve's game character looked exactly like Steve himself.

They hadn't been asked to pick or design characters. The game had just started after they selected their weapons, and suddenly they were inside the game as themselves. The machine must have taken photographs of them and created their own CGI characters. It made sense, but it was still kind of creepy. That just wasn't how most video games worked. Part of the fun of the game was getting to be someone else, to be a superhero or villain, a street-fighter, a gangster, a spy, or a hard-boiled detective. A game that just lets you be yourself within a virtual reality was unheard of.

It made the violence more personal, more real, and less ... virtual.

Marshall blocked the front door with his Uzi, mowing down anyone who tried to escape. A backdoor opened and he heard padded footsteps hurry down the back steps. As he dashed through the kitchen to the back door, in the corner of his eye he saw Steve's avatar grab a woman by her hair and drag her to the floor, ripping off her clothes. That's when he remembered what Crazy Cal had said about the game: "You can even rape bitches in this thing!"

Marshall paused and looked back, watching, half-mesmerized as Steve's game character pushed a woman down to her knees and forced her to give him a blowjob with a gun pressed to her temple.

"Suck this dick, bitch! Take it all down your throat!"

The woman in the game complied, slobbering on his erection while Steve fucked her throat aggressively. Marshall felt like he should have been more outraged, more disgusted, but instead, he felt himself getting aroused. From the moment he'd kicked in the door of this house, he'd been hoping he'd get to see some naked women, some titties maybe, but this was so, so much better, and yet so much worse.

He heard Steve cum with a stuttering moan, his body stiffening and jerking spasmodically as he pulled his cock from the whore's mouth and hosed her face with semen. Steve smiled, a look that was so inhumanly deranged it belonged on a B-movie serial killer, not his best friend, then he pointed the gun at the center of the whore's forehead and pulled the trigger, voiding her brains from her skull onto the warped and splintering hardwood floor.

"Oh, shit! My God, Steve!"

"Did you see that shit? It was fucking awesome! I could almost feel her lips on my dick for real, like she was really sucking it. I think I just came on myself, yo!"

Marshall was shaking, horrified by what he'd just witnessed and even more horrified by the erection tenting the front of his jeans. Even his game character had an erection. Marshall wanted a blowjob too, and that made him feel wretched, loathsome, like the crack dealers in his neighborhood who would ask crackwhores to bring their young daughters around for sex in exchange for a few rocks. He had to remind himself that no matter how realistic it seemed, it was just a video game, so it didn't matter what terrible immoral things they did or to whom. It didn't matter if they raped, murdered, tortured, and mutilated a dozen women. That was the purpose of the game. But the longer Marshall played, the more it felt like the game was changing him, eroding the moral and ethical walls civilization had built between humanity and its bestial, carnal, bloodthirsty genetic past, turning him into someone he didn't want to be, someone he could no longer recognize. If violent video games like Grand Theft Auto had been associated with lowered empathy and an increased proclivity toward violence in its players, this game seemed to be designed specifically to create violent sociopaths and psychopaths. It was a graphically illustrated journey through the mind of a mass murderer, slaughter as entertainment, a journey that would alter the brain patterns of the player, perhaps permanently. Marshall felt this, recognized it as it was happening, but could not pull himself away, could not stop playing.

Abandoning the runners who'd escaped out the back door, Marshall decided to check upstairs. He could hear female voices coming from the second floor, screaming for help. There was the sound of broken glass, then heavy footsteps racing down the steps. Marshall raised the Uzi, and when the big muscle-bound guy with the blue bandanna tied around his face and the M-16 assault rifle in his hands rounded the corner, Marshall put thirty or forty shells in the man's torso, spraying him with a shower of bullets. The big guy danced on the end of the spray like a kite in a rainstorm. Bright red holes blossomed like a field of roses all over his chest and torso. Marshall stepped aside as the man's body tumbled down the stairs. He picked up the M-16 where it had landed, exchanging the Uzi for it.

More police sirens were coming, adding to the cacophony of noise. Marshall made it to the second-floor landing and looked down the hall to his left; there were two bedrooms on one side and a bathroom across from those. At the other end of the hall to his right was another bedroom with the door shut tight. Marshall went right. He kicked in the door, then stepped through, raising the M-16. Two women sat huddled in the corner. One, a woman with dark skin that was so dry it had turned ashy gray and looked like reptile scales, a fraying weave, cracked ashen lips, and sagging tits sat with her legs spread wide, her unshaven sex gaping unselfconsciously, eyes glazed, a needle still dangling from her arm. To her left, hugging tight to her, was a girl roughly Marshall's age. She had a black eye and a bruise on her cheek. Her clothes had been torn, and she was struggling to hold the front of her ripped sundress closed over her large breasts. She had dimples that were prominent even while she was crying and big bright watery brown eyes. Her skin was smooth, brown, and unblemished where it had not been bruised by whatever sadistic trick had used her that day. It was a mother and her teenaged daughter. Their story was clear from their surroundings and condition. The mother had brought her daughter there to trade her for drugs or introduce her to the family business.

"Mom! Mom, help! Help me! Don't let him kill me!"

The girl tugged at her catatonic mother as he walked forward with the rifle raised. The tears streaming down her face were real. The fear in her eyes was real. It was then that Marshall realized he could smell the sulfur, the blood, the sweat, the ass, semen, and sour pussy funk that filled the house like a dank fog. This wasn't just a game. A part of him had known it all along. No game had graphics this realistic. All of this was real. Every bit of it. They were killing real people, but that was impossible.

"Don't worry. I won't hurt you," Marshall said as he continued to walk toward her, unbuttoning his pants.

"Yeah, fuck the shit out that whore! I got your back!" Steve yelled out from somewhere behind him as Marshall pinned the girl down, ripped open her dress, and brutally penetrated her, thrusting aggressively, feeling the tight wetness around his engorged cock, the girl's screams in his ears, her tears against his cheek, the smell of her hair products, her sweat, her sex. He wept as he raped her, knowing the line he had crossed. Somehow, this was even worse than killing the pregnant woman and her child. He'd always been taught that a rapist was the lowest thing you can be besides a child molester. Now, he had become that lowly repugnant thing. As he came, ejaculating his seed in the torn and bleeding vagina of this beautiful young girl who'd done nothing to deserve being abused and violated except being born to a mother who loved the needle more than her own flesh and blood, Marshall ripped off the virtual reality goggles, but he was still there, still in that room, still on top of the girl as she screamed and pleaded with him to stop. He still had the switchblade in his pocket, the one he'd used to disembowel Fat Sid. Marshall pulled it out and drew it slowly across the screaming girl's throat while he simultaneously pumped out the last of his seed deep within her.

"Yo, Marshall. The game's over. It's over, dog."

Marshall looked over at Steve who was grinning like a monkey with a fistful of shit. He'd taken his goggles off too, and was snapping his fingers in front of Marshall's face. Big letters on the video game screen spelled out "GAME OVER".

"Sorry, man. I must have spaced out for a minute. It was like I was still inside the game."

"That game was pretty fucking dope, huh?"

He looked at his best friend and started to stammer out a reply when the SWAT team rushed into the arcade.

"Get down! Get down! Hands behind your head! Drop the weapons!"

Marshall looked down at the knife in his hand. It was covered with blood, so was the machete at his feet and the ax leaning beside Steve.

"We didn't do anything!" Steve cried out as he crawled out of his chair and dropped to his knees on the floor with his fingers laced behind his head. "It was just a couple bags of candy. Fucking chill, yo!"

But Marshall knew this had nothing to do with candy.

"We have the shooters in custody," one of the policemen said.

Another officer grabbed Steve by the back of the neck and punched him in the stomach before slamming him hard against the floor and putting a knee in his back.

"You murdered over a dozen people! You killed police officers. I should blow your fucking head off right now!" the officer said, putting his Glock 9mm against Steve's temple and gritting his teeth, fighting the urge to murder him right there in front of everyone.

Marshall was shoved to the floor, practically tackled by two burly officers. His arms were jerked behind his back so hard he felt his shoulder pop as he was handcuffed.

"It was just a game. We were just playing a game. It wasn't real!" Marshall said, looking around for Crazy Cal. "Tell 'em, Cal! Tell 'em we didn't kill nobody! Tell 'em we was just playin' a video game!"

Cal stood leaning against the change machine, holding the bags of candy the two boys had stolen, reaching into the bags and pulling out handfuls of chocolate, shoveling them into his mouth wrappers and all. A kid with a huge Afro that was smashed flat in the front, wearing a Superman costume, stood beside him, holding a bag of ice to his forehead and staring murderously at Marshall. It was then Marshall remembered that one of the locations in the video game had been a police station. The kid smiled at him as if reading his mind.

"It was just a game," Marshall repeated as much to the kid

in the Superman costume as the cops sitting on his back, twisting his arms into the handcuffs.

"We've got you and your friend on video shooting those cops! Murdering that pregnant woman! Killing kids! You two sick pieces of shit are going to burn in hell for this! You're going straight to death row!"

"It was just a video game!" Marshall shouted again, staring at Crazy Cal's weird, thin-lipped, chocolate-stained, smile, now convinced that those who believed G-town existed somewhere in hell were right.

Chapter Five

SEVEN YEARS

Seven years ago, my best friend Greg died. Shot down in the street. Seven years ago, I fired a gun for the last time. Seven years ago, I vowed never to live that type of life again, I vowed to change. And I did. I'm not that angry young man I used to be.

The guy with the gray hoodie was following me again. His pants sagged low, past his hips, so you could see his red and white Calvin Klein boxers–and the gun in his waistband. He kept his head bent down, staring at the sidewalk beneath his old-school black and white high-top Nikes. His face was hidden by the hood, enshrouded in shadows. Hands shoved deep into the pockets of his faded black jeans, which were at least two sizes too big. He kept a respectable distance, but this was the second day I'd seen him following behind me. It wasn't a coincidence. He was after me.

Adrenaline dumped into my bloodstream like a blast of crack cocaine. My heartbeat quickened. I could hear it. Feel it pounding against my chest, trying to free itself from the prison of my ribcage. My breath came fast and hard. The edges of my vision began to close in, narrowing to a fist-sized window. I hadn't felt this in years. It was the fight or flight response, my body preparing itself for danger. I used to get this feeling four or five times a day when I was younger. Before I changed.

Seven years ago, I was a street thug, a gangsta. I sold drugs, carried a gun, even used it a few times. I was headed for destruction. Then I decided I wanted to go to college. Now, I'm two months away from graduating from The University of Pennsylvania with a neuroscience degree–unless I get shot first.

The guy behind me looked over his shoulder. His head swiveled, looking from one side of the street to the other, scanning for witnesses. Making sure no one would be able to identify him once whatever he had planned for me went down, and scoping out his exit route. I knew the routine. I'd done it many times myself. I even knew what he was thinking, all the psychological games he was playing to push his conscience to the side, lower his inhibitions, and silence his fear. Telling himself he was a "bad motherfucker", that this would be an easy mark. I was determined not to be. I needed a weapon.

This area of town wasn't like the hood I grew up in. There were no broken bottles or pieces of rubble and debris from buildings that had crumbled, burnt out, or been looted. No random car parts sitting on someone's front yard or just lying there on the sidewalk. This was Society Hill. I worked at a clothing store here during the week to help pay for my books and supplies. It was all brick homes with manicured lawns, opulent apartment buildings with doormen, five star restaurants, and extravagant boutiques. Mercedes, BMWs, and the occasional Cadillac or expensive SUV passed me on the street, always within a mile or two of the speed limit. It was clean and safe. At least it was normally. That left few options for improvised self-defense weapons. I didn't like my chances of taking on an armed assailant with nothing but my fists. I hadn't thrown down with anyone in years. Not since I got my life in order and enrolled in college. I couldn't remember the last time I had to bust some fool's grill with nothing but my fists. That wasn't who I was anymore.

Changing the entire trajectory of my life hadn't been as simple as waking up one day and deciding I wanted a better life for myself, but then again, it was. It was Sunday morning, seven years ago almost to the day, when the idea to do something different with my life first came to me. I had attended my best friend Greg's funeral the morning before. I watched his mother wail and scream over his coffin, repeating "Why?" to the listless air above the church and crying out for her baby, insane with grief. I imagined my own mother grieving over my coffin the same way. My death would ruin her. But I knew that's how my life would likely end. Few young black men made it out of the ghetto alive. That's just something I grew to accept like corrupt cops stopping me on the street and searching me without probable cause, bill collectors calling all hours of the day, white Jesus's, and black republicans.

Greg had been sitting right next to me at the bus stop when he got shot. A drive-by. A guy in a black Cutlass Supreme leaning out the passenger side window with a red scarf wrapped around his face, black sunglasses, and an AR-15 on full auto. For all I know, those bullets had been intended for me. I dove behind a car, landing face-first on the concrete, busting my lip, chipping my front tooth, and gashing open my forehead. Greg landed directly in front of the bench we'd been sitting on. Half his skull was missing. Blood poured from his ears and nose like a fountain of red wine gushing down into the gutter. He was gone. A kid I'd known since kindergarten, who I'd just been laughing with moments before, was now a bleeding sack of meat. That's when I knew I had to change my life. Still, it was almost another month before I actually took action. My high school science teacher, Mr. Sumpter, was the one who finally convinced me to do something about my future.

I was sitting in science class, thinking about Greg, anxious for the lunch bell to ring so I could sell the ten vials of crack in my coat pocket before the school police decided to single me out for a "random" search. I had been daydreaming about a conversation Greg and I had right before he'd gotten his skull hollowed out. It was the last time Greg and I laughed together.

"I read this article the other day that has me trippin'. That shit was deep, yo."

"Hold up. Hold up. You mean, your ass can read?" Greg joked.

"I'm serious, man. Listen!"

"All right, all right. What's up?"

"So, it was this article about how every seven years, each cell in your body is reproduced except for like a few neurons in the center of your brain, your cerebral cortex. You become like an entirely new person. You still got all the memories of the person you used to be. Same personality. Same perspective on shit. You look the same, act the same, got the same scars, same fears, same hopes. You might be like a little taller or fatter or skinnier than the dude you were seven years ago. Maybe your hair is longer or grayer. You know I'm sayin'? You still feel like you, but you ain't you. You're like a whole different you. You know I'm sayin'? You share hardly any cells in common with that dude you were seven years ago. So, what happens to that motherfucker you used to be? Where do they go?"

Greg smiled. His fat cheeks exploded with dimples. I knew he was about to say something ridiculous.

"I don't know, fool. Maybe they go to your momma's house!"

We had both fallen over, holding our sides as we laughed our asses off.

I couldn't help letting out a little chuckle as I recalled the moment. Mr. Sumpter cleared his throat, and I looked up to see him standing above my desk. Mr. Sumpter was six-eight.

He'd been a basketball star at Temple University back in the eighties. Now he was in his fifties, a head full of salt and pepper dreadlocks, wrinkles at the corners of his eyes, but could still dunk a basketball and outrun most of the guys on the school track team.

"'Sup, Mr. S?"

He slapped my science mid-term down on the desk in front of me. I gawked at the grade. 100. Mr. Sumpter looked down at me and just shook his head like it was the worst possible score rather than the best. He walked past me, handing out a few more tests. Then he paused and looked back at me.

"You know what gets me, Mr. Brown?"

Mr. Sumpter always called us by our last names, adding "Mr.", "Mrs.", "Sir", and "Ma'am" as if he were addressing peers rather than a bunch of badass, hard-headed students.

"What up, Mr. S?"

"You're one of the smartest kids in this class. You pass the tests without even trying. I know you don't study. But you have the worst grades in the class because you don't do your homework. You don't turn in your papers when they're due. You hardly come to class. You just don't care."

"At least my grades ain't as bad as Tyrell's. He can't even spell his name right."

All the other kids in the class began to laugh. A big, thick-necked kid with biceps the same size as his head jumped up, knocking over his desk.

"Fuck did you say 'bout me, nigga?"

I met his eyes. Not getting out of my seat but reaching into my jacket, where I would have normally been carrying my Glock 9mm. It wasn't there. It was in my car. They had metal detectors in the school now. But it didn't matter. Tyrell got the message.

"I said you stupid as fuck. But if you think all them muscles can stop a bullet, go ahead and do sumpin'. Otherwise, you betta sit your big ass down before you get put down."

Mister Sumpter let out a long sigh then just shook his head again.

"You know, Mr. Brown, you're a Junior. Next year you'll be graduating and doing what? Do you even know what you're going to do after high school? Hang out on the street with your hoodlum friends doing nothing? Selling drugs? Fighting? You could be going to college in two years on a full academic scholarship. You know that? You're smart enough. If you spent half as much time doing homework as you do trying to be hard and intimidate everybody, you'd be school valedictorian. Instead, you'll probably wind up dead or in prison."

Dead or in prison.

I'd heard some variation of that shit all my life. It was the destiny of all young black males according to the media and our so-called mentors. I'd always accepted it as fate. And once accepted, it became a self-fulfilling prophecy.

Dead or in prison.

But now, after seeing Greg die, it was like it finally sank in, and I didn't want to die. That night I did my homework. I flushed all the crack vials I had left down the toilet and didn't re-up. From then on, I dedicated myself to schoolwork. Four months later, I made the high school honor roll. The next year, as a senior, I made honor roll all four quarters. I didn't make valedictorian, but I did get that academic scholarship to University of Penn and moved to Philadelphia. From a Baltimore ghetto to an Ivy League campus. The culture shock felt like an electrocution, but I adapted. After I graduated from Penn, my plan was to go straight to med school. Then, two nights ago, I saw that guy in the gray hoodie standing on a street corner, watching me. I knew it was the same guy. He was dressed exactly as he is now. Same walk. Same shifty, suspicious mannerisms.

I crossed the street, casting a glance over my shoulder in time to see the guy in the hood cross also, less than half a block behind me. I wished I had a gun with me too, but I had given up that type of life. The 9mm I used to carry was in a Nike shoebox in the closet of my old bedroom back at my momma's house in Baltimore. Violence was my past. If I wanted to be a different person, it meant leaving all that shit behind. You can't live in two worlds at the same time. But it would have been nice to have my gat at that moment.

There was an alley ahead. One thing I had learned on the streets long ago was that the only way an unarmed man had a chance against someone who was strapped was in close quarters. Close enough to grab the guy's gun or hit him with something and hopefully knock him unconscious. Distance favored the guy who could spit bullets. I needed to draw him in close to survive this.

I ducked into the alley between two apartment buildings and pressed myself against the wall, trying to blend into the shadows. Taking one last look around for something I could use as a weapon, I spotted a dumpster. There was a chain on it, but it was unlocked. The lock was just dangling there. In three long strides, I was across the alley, pulling the chain and the lock free, feeling now like I actually had a realistic chance of surviving this. I returned to my spot on the wall, trying to make myself invisible again, hoping the guy in the hoodie would just pass right by the alley and keep walking but knowing instinctively that he wouldn't.

The last time I'd been hiding in an alley waiting to ambush someone was when Greg and I planned to rob a kid, a mule who carried drugs and money back and forth to a stash house in my old neighborhood in Baltimore. It had been Greg's idea–kinda. Greg told me about the kid. I was the one who suggested gankin' him, just runnin' up on him and sticking a gun in the kid's face when he was on his way back to the stash house after making his rounds. When he'd be flush with either drugs or cash. We didn't care which. We'd snatch his backpack and disappear before he knew who or what hit him.

We both had on ski-masks despite the hot-ass, eighty-five-degree May weather. I can remember the kid's face when I put the barrel of that Glock against the bridge of his nose. He was barely a teenager. Thirteen? Fourteen? Maybe just a twelve-year-old who was big for his age. He had a face full of pimples and baby fat on his cheeks. His eyes had gone from wide with shock to furious with rage. No fear. It wasn't what we'd been expecting.

It all happened so fast. Isn't that what they always say? Victims and perpetrators alike? It all happened so fast. As if things might have been different had they transpired at a slower pace. As if a few seconds might have spared that kid's life.

The kid lifted his shirt, reached into his waistband. I saw the handle of his pistol, a Glock 9mm. Just like mine. What the hell was a kid that age doing with a Glock and not some shitty little second-hand revolver? This kid was carrying a brand-spanking new nine-hundred-dollar semi-automatic handgun. I watched his bony little hand seize the hilt, and then I pulled the trigger ... and just a few hours later, Greg was dead too. Maybe the kid following me had something to do with that night? Maybe he'd come all the way from Baltimore to find me? Revenge on that pimple-faced mule's remaining murderer. He might even have been the same one who'd murdered Greg. Maybe that kid we'd killed was his brother or cousin or part of his gang? I know that if someone shot one of my family members in the face, driving a few states away to find his killer and end his life would have been nothing at all, even seven years later.

I was sweating, breathing like I'd just run a marathon. My hands were shaking, and things were getting blurry. I was about to pass out. I took long deep breaths to slow my breathing and heart rate. This was the wrong time for my first panic attack. I had to pull my shit together.

Then the guy turned the corner into the alley ... and reached for his gun. I swung the lock and chain and caught him on the temple. The gun almost fell from his hands. He juggled it from hand to hand, then crushed it against his chest as he went down hard, falling backwards against the brick building, bouncing off and dropping to the filthy cement floor on his side, then rolling to his back. But he never dropped the gun. I was preparing to swing the lock again when he raised it and pulled the trigger.

The sound was deafening. Like an explosion rather than a gunshot. The walls of the alley echoed the sound like a mini-amphitheater. The blast buzzed in my ears, an angry hornet stinging my eardrums. I felt the punch of the bullet as it struck my chest, a raindrop through tissue paper, tearing straight through my torso without resistance. My next breath gurgled with blood and burned like I was breathing ash. The bullet had struck a lung. I was fucked.

I looked down at my assailant, my murderer. The impact of the lock had left a large bloody gash from above his left temple to the center of his forehead. His left eye was almost glued shut from all the blood dripping down his face, but I recognized him.

At first, I thought it was that same kid Greg and I murdered seven years ago. Somehow, that's who I'd been expecting it to be. A vengeful spirit here to drag me to hell with it. But ghosts don't bleed. This was no spirit. It wasn't the mule we'd shot. It wasn't Greg come back from beyond eternity to seek his own revenge against the one indirectly responsible for his untimely death. My unresolved guilt almost welcomed such an end. I was certain his death and the robbery/homicide I dragged him into were connected.

The face looking back at me, grinning triumphantly through a dripping red mask, was almost alien in the way that mundane creatures can appear exotic and bizarre when placed in incongruous environments. A crow flitting through the halls of a hospital. A stray dog wandering from classroom to classroom. An infant in a strip club. A nun in a crack house.

My own teenaged face looking up at me from the alley floor. I had killed me. It made no sense.

"Why?" I mouthed, unable to get enough air into my punctured lungs to form words. The kid smiled at me. My smile. The one I'd had seven years ago before I'd gotten the chipped tooth in the front capped.

"Dead or in prison," he replied. My fate, spoken to me without explanation, because none was needed.

They say that every seven years, each cell in your body is reproduced except for a scant few neurons in your cerebral cortex. You become an entirely new person. You may have all the memories of the person you used to be. Same personality. Same perspective on the world. You may be similar in appearance, share the same scars. Maybe you're a little taller or fatter, or skinnier than the person you were seven years ago. Maybe your hair is longer or grayer. Perhaps you have acquired new scars or wrinkles. You still feel like you, but you aren't. You share hardly any cells in common with that person you were seven years ago. So, what happens to that person? Where do they go?

You may have become an entirely new person. But the old you, the one that knows your secrets, your sins, never goes away. And sometimes, he catches up with you. I thought I'd escaped my destiny. That I'd changed from the killer I used to be. But that killer had found me.

With the dimming embers of my vitality, I swung the heavy lock down onto that motherfucker's skull, once, twice, and a third half-hearted swing with no strength behind it that splashed down into the bloody pulp the first two impacts had made of my murderer's brain pan and stuck there. The lock fit neatly in the yawning fissure in his skull like a bizarre cosmetic accessory. An extreme piercing or surgical body modification glinting in the moonlight.

My lungs were collapsing, filling with blood, but I managed to squeak out a few hoarse words before losing consciousness. The same words my younger self had said to me before blowing a hole in my chest. The same words I'd heard all of my life.

"Dead or in prison."

I knew my limits, and there was no way my 16-year-old self would have survived prison.

Chapter Six

THE ECSTASY OF AGONY

I feared her
dimples and double Ds
cute
sexy
sweet
sensitive
loving
affectionate
Karma in a short black skirt
an imminent heartbreak

I feared her
as she smiled
as she held my hand
as she climbed into my lap
as she kissed me
as I felt her breasts
those big, supple, perfect breasts

I feared her
as she reached down

and stroked my cock
as my fingers found
the wet warmth
at the center of her
as she bowed her head
between my legs
took me in her mouth
and made me growl

I feared her
as she straddled me
slid my manhood
up inside her
in and out of her
in the front seat of my car
in the parking lot
of the restaurant
where we'd just met

I feared her
as I took her from behind
bent over my car seat
as I laid her on the back seats
entered her aggressively
savagely
desperate with need and desire
the hunger of a predator
after too many unsuccessful hunts
as I parted her thighs
tasted her
made her legs quiver and clench my cheeks

I feared her
as she cried out
with the force of her climax
As I mounted her again

thrusting like an animal
toward my own orgasm

I feared her
as I erupted onto her belly
I feared her
as I collapsed on top of her
snuggled against her
kissed her face
kissed her throat
kissed her breasts
Nuzzled in the nape of her neck
my armor gone for a moment
vulnerable as a hermit crab
between shells

And isn't misogyny
just another name for fear?
Isn't this rage inside me
just an unhealed wound?
Another word for sadness
with no other way to express itself?
Isn't this blade
just a substitute for my own erection
diminishing against her belly?
The thrusting of it into her carotid artery
another way to fuck her throat?
Another way to hear her moan my name?

My heaving sobs
another way to show my love for her?

Her slow death
another way to keep her
forever?

The knife in my own heart
another way to give her
my soul?

The agony of it all
another form of ecstasy?

Chapter Seven

BIG GAME HUNTER

The rusty old hatchback wheezed and rattled, belching clouds of exhaust as it chugged through the snowstorm, slipping and sliding through the thick slush coating the streets. Emotionless eyes peered through a swirling curtain of white, searching the pedestrians for him.

Stan didn't know exactly who he was because he hadn't selected him yet. Maybe he would be the man in the combat boots and the big, puffy, navy blue coat with the fake fur lining the hood hurrying along the sidewalk with his head down and a scarf wrapped around his face so only his eyes were visible. Or the man in the motorcycle jacket, the leather Muir cap, and the equestrian boots stepping out of the cab and practically skipping into the vestibule of the bar across the street with the foreboding name, The Bear Trap. How ominously appropriate. Or the huge man in the black jeans and Timberland work boots, wearing a black leather bomber jacket. He sported a black lumberjack beard and thick bushy eyebrows. He was well over six feet tall and approaching three hundred pounds. Stan couldn't tell what his body was like, but he could imagine. A powerlifter's physique, big muscular chest and shoulders, huge biceps and triceps, an equally large belly, and titanic thighs that could crush a man's skull. Muscle and fat in equal proportion, covered in a wispy layer of soft black hair. A bear. A muscle bear, specifically. Just what Stan was looking for.

He couldn't actually be certain what the man really looked like beneath his jacket. How much was wishful thinking, his own fantasies coloring his perceptions, and how much was reality. The tight-fitting jeans the man wore definitely showed massive, muscular thighs. This was a man who had done more than a few squats and deadlifts, probably with twice Stan's own one-hundred-and-eighty-pound bodyweight. And the bomber jacket he wore didn't do much to hide his belly. Stan could extrapolate that a guy who spent that much time doing squats probably spent equal time on the weight bench. The guy knew his way around a gym. He was just clearly not into cardio or dieting. Which was also just perfect.

Stan pulled up alongside him and rolled down his window.

"Need a ride?"

The big bearded man leaned down to peer through the passenger window of Stan's Subaru Outback. Assessing Stan's vanilla appearance, a white button-up shirt, red cardigan sweater with a red knitted scarf and red mittens, hair perfectly coiffed, big dorky smile. He must have looked like a gay Mister Rogers. The big man scowled, shook his head, and chuckled.

"You ain't my type, buddy. And I'm already where I'm going," he said with a sneer, gesturing toward The Bear Trap.

"Okay. Just trying to be helpful. Stay safe."

Stan rolled up his window and drove off. He had made his choice. He was the one.

When he was a kid, just eleven years old, his father took little Stanley hunting for the first time. This was one of the many "masculine" activities that were supposed to make a man of his effeminate son who had no affinity for and absolutely abhorred sports of all kinds. It had taken his father months to finally accept that his son would never be a football or baseball player. Catching Stan playing doctor under the bleachers with another boy had finally convinced his father to let him drop out of football, but his dad wasn't giving up.

The following weekend, Stan's father took him camping by a lake so they could go fishing together. Stan had no idea why his father thought fishing was so masculine, but that's what they did. Maybe his dad thought just spending a day alone together would do the trick, some quality father/son time. Stan did enjoy the time with his father, until he got drunk and began yelling at the fish for not biting and at Stan for not wanting to put worms on the hook himself and recoiling at the suggestion that he should be the one to take the hook from the mouth of the one fish his father managed to reel in. Then, when Stan finally caught one and his dad helped him reel it in, his father yelled at him when he squealed at the wet, wriggling thing and dropped it back into the lake. So, hunting it was.

The hunting trip wasn't just Stan and his dad. A bunch of his father's friends came along. Stan's "uncles." Jimmy and Elmo, two of his father's old army buddies. Stanley, his father's roommate in college. Charles, the guy who owned the neighborhood butcher shop and who was on the dart team at his dad's favorite bar. And Simon, a guy his dad worked with at the Ford factory. Oh, and his real uncle, Micky. Or, as his father liked to call him, his mother's "idiot brother."

It was near the end of deer hunting season, and they all drove to the campsite in their own trucks, Rams, F150s, and Chevy Silverados, lifted, with gun racks and tires as tall as a second-grader. They quickly pitched tents within yards of a "deer blind" that was high up in the tree and had a makeshift, rickety-looking ladder as tall as a two-story house. Little Stanley trembled at the prospect of climbing that thing. Luckily, his father had other plans.

"You and me are going to track us a deer, not sit up in a

deer blind like those idiots, drinking beer, jacking off, and waiting for one to wander by."

They stalked through the woods, following deer tracks, footprints, shrubs that Stanley's father showed him had been chewed on, and the occasional droppings. Frequently, his father admonished him for being too noisy, even though Stanley hadn't said a word and was doing his best to step as carefully as possible. But it was autumn. The forest floor was littered with fallen leaves. He wasn't a damn ninja. How was he not supposed to crunch an occasional leaf or twig? But Stanley knew better than to argue. He just nodded and silently mouthed "Sorry." His father responded by rolling his eyes and shaking his head as if he couldn't understand how he'd spawned such a moron.

Finally, they spotted a deer. His father made a few hand gestures, most of which Stan did not understand. But he got the most important ones. Stop. Look over there. Get low. Shut the fuck up.

Stanley's father passed him the hunting rifle, A Smith & Wesson M&P 15 300 Whisper. It had a 1:75 twist ratio, 5R rifling, gas block with Picatinny rail, forged trigger guard, chromed firing pin, painted with an APG camo. Stanley knew all of that because his father had repeated those unnecessary details more than half a dozen times during their drive to the campsite, and at least twice that morning. Stanley found most of what his father said when it came to guns completely indecipherable, a coded message for which he lacked the encryption key.

The deer hadn't moved. His father pointed the gun in the general direction of the deer and guided him to press his eye to the scope while simultaneously arranging Stanley's hands into the proper grip before standing back and gesturing for Stanley to shoot. Stanley took a deep breath, closed his eyes, then slowly opened them, focusing on the rifle's crosshairs and the deer beyond them. He exhaled slowly and pulled the trigger, being certain not to jerk or flinch on the recoil, which would have brought a volley of derision from his father, who already thought he was a pussy.

His shot hit the deer right behind the shoulder, just like his father taught him. The deer fell and lay still, not twitching or spasming, just dead. It was a heart shot. His father's jaw dropped.

"Holy shit! That was perfect!"

He scooped his son up and gave the boy a huge hug.

"I think we found your sport, son. That was probably the best shot I've ever seen. I completely botched it the first time my dad took me hunting. I shot the damn thing in the ass and it took off running. My dad laughed his ass off. No matter how many deer I got after that, he would always tell everyone who would listen how I shot a deer in the ass. You're a much better shot than I ever was."

That was the first time his father ever praised him. His dad was right, Stanley had found his sport. And he found something else that trip when his mother's idiot brother took him on a walk in the woods that evening after his father passed out drunk and showed him how to give a blowjob and how good they felt to receive. The next night, his uncle Mickey introduced him to Astroglide and the joy of prostate massage and anal orgasms, followed by an even more intimate intrusion that left Stanley walking bowlegged and wincing when he sat.

That weekend, and many more such hunting trips with Uncle Mickey, inextricably bound sex and hunting together in Stanley's mind and libido. Whenever Stanley fantasized, it was about big hairy men, hunting rifles, blood, and semen. Just a few months ago, he finally put it all together with his first bear hunt.

His first was an accident ... of sorts. He didn't accidentally shoot the man. He didn't accidentally fuck the man while he bled out on the asphalt in the parking lot of the gay nightclub downtown. He didn't accidentally ejaculate deep in the dying man's bowels while listening to his death rattle. It was walking into that nightclub in the first place that was the accident. It was seeing the big man with the big biceps and the big hairy chest dancing up on stage dressed as a slutty nouveau Village People construction worker that was the accident. It was feeling the arousal and the bloodlust rise in him when he realized how much the man resembled his late Uncle Mickey that was the accident. Following the man out to the parking lot after last call had been calculated. Putting the gun to his back and putting a hole through his lungs had been deliberate. Yanking down his tight jeans and revealing his tight, muscular ass had been deliberate. Lubricating his cock with the man's blood and sliding it in his rectum as the man thrashed and convulsed, lungs filling with blood, drowning and gasping for air ... that had all been deliberate. As deliberate as Stan circling the block and pulling into the Bear Trap's parking lot. As deliberate as following the big man in the black leather bomber jacket into the bar and watching him from across the room. Watching him dance with other men. Watching him aggressively kiss a young twink in tight neon green shorts before shoving the little man away like he was tossing away an empty beer can. This man was every bit the alpha. He was the most rawly, unpretentiously masculine creature Stan had ever seen. He had to have him.

In Stan's mind, fucking another man was true alpha-male shit. Especially when one of them looked like Atlas holding up the world. He imagined such men were too masculine for any woman. That it would take a true man to take on such a behemoth. The type of man Stan always wanted to be.

"Can I buy you a drink?" A well-dressed man in his late twenties, in skin-tight Calvin Klein skinny jeans, a crisp yellow Ralph Lauren Polo shirt, with a lean athletic build and chiseled matinee-idol looks stepped between Stan and his view of the big bear.

Stan had the urge to shove the man out of the way. Instead, he smiled politely and said, "No, thank you." It would not do to be intoxicated when attempting to take down such large prey.

"But, I insist," the man said, smiling his biggest Colgate smile and batting the bluest eyes Stan had ever seen.

"I am not interested. Sorry, you just aren't my type."

"Oh, come on. I'm everyone's type," the man replied, refusing to take the hint.

"And how many of Jeffrey Dahmer's victims do you imagine said that exact same thing?"

Perhaps it was his cryptic words, the pitiless look in Stan's eyes, or his obnoxious red cardigan, but the man finally decided to flirt elsewhere.

"Fucking weirdo," the man said, as he turned and walked away. Stan felt profound, almost euphoric satisfaction in shooting down the advances of someone so conceited, so convinced of his own attractiveness and desirability. It took him a moment, but he managed to locate the bear again. He was locking lips with another burly man in leather. Stanley felt pangs of jealousy, fear, and excitement. Two of them would make a challenging hunt and an amazing prize, fuel for months of masturbatory fantasies. The risk would be more than worth the reward.

Stanley stalked them around the club. It felt very much like hunting. He did his best to blend in with the crowd. His red sweater wasn't exactly camouflage, but he kept as safe a distance as he could, peering at the couple through the dense forest of sweating bodies in leather. He watched them embrace several times, grabbing and groping asses and crotches as they kissed. Stan felt that now familiar mix of jealousy and lust each time the two big men came together in passion. Finally, the two made their way toward the exit, with Stan following behind, unnoticed in the crowd.

Stan had his gun in a holster in his waistband, a Desert Eagle .50 caliber. A big gun for big prey. But Stan didn't want them dead yet. Once in the parking lot, he sprinted to his car to grab his CO_2 rifle and a handful of tranquilizer darts loaded with a combination of Valium, Ketamine, and Dilaudid. He kept the Desert Eagle on him just in case things went south. He raced back in the direction of the couple, hoping they were still together and hadn't already gotten in their vehicles.

He spotted the big guy in the leather motorcycle jacket and leather pants, but not his original prey. Stan felt a moment of disappointment but realized he was just being greedy. Trying to take on two big men was reckless. That's the type of irrational, emotional thinking that would get him caught. This would be safer, more practical. He fumbled a dart into the air rifle, almost injecting himself in the process, then crept toward the man in leather. He wasn't the one Stan really wanted, but he would do.

As the man fumbled with his keys, Stan rose from where he was crouched between a big sedan and a midsize SUV, pointed the air rifle at the man, and carefully lined up the sights. He took a deep breath and held it, aiming for a spot directly above the man's right shoulder but below his prominent jawline. His neck. If he could get the dart in the man's jugular or carotid, it was a quicker path to the brain for the tranq dart, and the sudden intrusion of a needle into his throat would hopefully choke off any cries for help.

Stan heard a door open somewhere behind him. Far enough away that it was probably not an issue, but he knew he should check. He was tempted to take the shot before turning to make sure there was no one watching him, but again, that would be reckless. If he didn't take the shot now, he might lose his prey. He struggled with the decision for a moment or two before turning with a frustrated sigh. There was a split second of puzzlement as his mind grappled with what he was seeing. Big, hairy knuckles filled his entire field of vision, then there was an impact that whipped his head back and sent him crashing to the asphalt, and Stan understood he'd been punched. He looked up to see the big man with the bomber jacket standing above him, raising his big leather boot and bringing it down to Stan's face for Stan to worship it, or so

Stan's concussed brain interpreted the action before sole of boot met point of chin and everything went black.

Stan awoke slowly. Everything was foggy and spinny, and his head hurt. He saw two large shadows stalking toward him.

"This homophobic piece of shit is awake."

"I'm not ... I'm not ..." Stan's voice trailed off as he fought his way to consciousness. His thoughts felt like they were swimming through mud. A hard smack brought things into better focus but increased the splitting pain in his skull.

"Wake the fuck up, you piece of shit. I drugged you with your own dart after I kicked your ass. You've been out for over an hour, you homophobic asshole!"

"I'm ... I'm not."

Another hard slap.

"You're not what?"

"I'm not a homophobe!"

The man held up Stan's pistol and the tranquilizer rifle.

"Then what were you going to do with these?"

The other man held up his murder kit: duct tape, rope, a ball gag, handcuffs, more tranquilizer darts, a small ax, and a bone saw.

"And, there's still a shovel and a bag of lye in your trunk. You were going to kill us, you homophobic piece of shit."

"I wasn't ... I'm not homophobic!"

"You mean you aren't afraid of gay people, you just hate them? Your stupid little bible told you to kill homosexuals?"

"I'm an atheist, for Christ's sake! And, I'm gay!"

That was the first time Stan had uttered those words to another living soul. He had to admit, there was something freeing in saying it out loud.

They looked confused for a moment, then the big bear who'd been wearing the bomber jacket, but was now wearing nothing more than a leather jockstrap and boots, stepped forward and grabbed Stan by the chin. The man's body was exactly as Stan had pictured it, huge shoulders the size of soccer balls with a chest to match, massive arms layered in thick muscle, thighs like tree trunks, and a big round belly that jutted out over his jockstrap, sticking out a good six inches in front of him. A thin downy coat of black hair coated his entire body.

"Did I fuck your boyfriend or something?"

"It's ... it's nothing like that," Stan said, hanging his head in shame. The big man lifted Stan's head, forcing him to make eye contact.

"Then what the fuck were you doing with all of this?" the other man asked. He was wearing big boots, but nothing else. He had a thick cock that was of average length and a body similar to the other man, though much less muscular and less hairy. Stan found himself unable to stop staring at the man's swinging cock. The big man followed his eyes, then smiled and let go of Stan's jaw.

"I guess you weren't lying. You're definitely gay. So, what the fuck's your problem? You just get off on killing big, burly gay men? That's it, isn't it? Oh, my God, that's it! That's what gets you off!"

"Don't kink shame me."

"Kink-shame? You're a fucking serial killer! You were going to kill Axel if I hadn't stopped you. That's not a fucking kink. That's a full-fledged twist, you twisted fuck!"

"I still feel like you're shaming me. That's not cool."

"Shaming you for being a fucking murderer!"

"Still not cool. I don't shame you for whatever you're into."

"You don't even know what I'm into."

Stan looked around. They were in a dungeon. A spanking bench, St Andrew's Cross, a stockade, a medical table, and countless floggers, whips, paddles, and oversized dildos cluttered the room.

"Everything I do is consensual."

"It's still hurting people."

The big man slapped him again.

"Don't you dare try to compare what you were about to do

to us with what we do! You're a fucking killer! You hunt gay people! You kill the very people you claim to identify with! Who fucked you up? Why do you hate us? Why do you hate yourself?"

Stan began to weep.

"I don't hate you. I love you! I think you're so beautiful!"

His crying increased into ugly pathetic, phlegmy, wheezing, whining, strangled, choking sounds. The big man backed away. He gestured toward his naked friend, and the two began to whisper.

"What are we going to do with this guy? I don't feel right torturing and killing him. I mean, when I thought he was some kind of Right-wing terrorist nut-job, I was ready to do my worst. But, I don't know. This feels wrong. The guy is in pain."

"How many people do you think he's killed, Ben? Didn't we hear about a guy going missing just last month? And then there was the guy who was shot and sodomized in the parking lot of Pirates. What if this is the guy who did it? We can't just let him go so he can go out there and kill more people. Maybe we should just turn him in to the police?"

"The police don't give a fuck about us. Besides, it will be our word against his, Axel. Our fingerprints are all over the guns now, and we are the ones who kidnapped him and brought him down here to my dungeon. It's not a good look."

"Fuck. What are we going to do, Ben?"

"I have an idea."

* * *

Stan looked out through the bars of his cage at his new Masters. He had always been attracted to big strong alpha males. The bigger and stronger the better. He knew it all stemmed from those hunting trips with his dad and Uncle Mickey. From the perspective of a little boy, Uncle Mickey had looked huge. He knew now that his uncle was an average-sized man, but his fantasies had exaggerated him into a gargantuan human, much like the leather-clad titans who now kept him as their pet.

Human beings are the only animals that keep other animals as pets. It's the ultimate expression of dominance, apex-predator shit. To keep an animal not as food, not as a slave to do work, but just as a toy, a plaything. Only humans, who stand at the top of the food chain, do that. And these two hulking alpha-males were proving their dominance over him by keeping him as their pet, and Stanley loved it.

Ben walked over to Stan's cage, where the ex-serial killer was gagged and in a leather hood with an o-ring gag and tiny nostril holes and zippered eyeholes. Ben zipped the eyeholes shut, trapping Stan in darkness. Stan's arms were bound behind his back in a leather bondage sleeve, and his ankles were shackled in steel cuffs. He shuffled forward and was led out of the cage on his knees by a leash attached to the collar around his neck and around the corner into another room. His Master removed his hood.

There were eight other men in the room in addition to his two Masters. They were all naked, all huge. His Master, Ben, was naked as well. His ten-inch cock jutted straight out like a spear. It was seven inches around, thick as Stan's wrist. Taking all of it in always left him bruised and bloody.

Ben reached down and grabbed Stan by the throat, forcing his cock down Stan's throat. Stan gagged and choked as his esophagus was brutally raped. Tears wept from his eyes. His other Master, Axel, took his position behind him, parted Stan's ass cheeks. He spit on his puckered anus, using the glob of saliva to ease his thick cock inside. He held a short snake-whip in his hand and began cracking it against Stan's back and shoulders, leaving welts and weals, turning his back into a roadmap of bleeding cuts as he and Ben fucked tears and moans and screams out of him. They took turns stretching his rectum before finally emptying themselves down Stan's throat.

"I'm going to let my friends have you for a few hours," Ben

announced as he drained his balls down his pet's gullet. "Some of these men were friends of two of the men you killed. They are going to use you, and they are going to hurt you. You won't fight, and you won't protest."

"Yes, Master."

He would be raped and beaten repeatedly that day and every day after that. But he would be happy. For the first time in his life, Little Stanley was happy.

Chapter Eight

UNSOLICITED

Marty lined up the energy drink beside his cock. It teetered on his thigh and fell to the floor a couple times before he managed to snap a photo with his cell phone. He didn't like how it looked. The curve in his penis made it appear smaller, less impressive, and impressive was what he was going for. He took a few more shots from various angles before getting just the right one, then quickly sent it to a friend of an online friend, Sheila Alfonso.

He'd never met her or had any interactions with her, and she certainly had never requested a surprise photo of his engorged man-meat. But she'd recently posted a few photos of herself on vacation in Cancun wearing a bikini. It caught Marty's eye. Her body was absolutely flawless. He was hoping he would catch her eye with his dick pics. Not that he'd ever received any positive results from sending unsolicited photos of his penis. But Marty couldn't help himself.

It was a compulsion. Perhaps a sickness. Marty hadn't spent much time speculating on it. Self-reflection wasn't really his thing. He just knew sending photos to anonymous women, and some not-so-anonymous, helped fuel his masturbatory fantasies. How it affected them didn't concern him, unless it inspired them to want to fuck.

He decided to up the ante and make a video. He turned on his webcam and aimed it at his cock as he began stroking it. He didn't like how his oversized belly flopped and jiggled, so Marty turned off the camera and went through his drawers, looking for the spandex waist trainer/ girdle he sometimes wore beneath his clothes to hold his belly in.

Marty sat down at his desk, turned the web camera back on, then focused it directly on his cock and balls. He zoomed in so his erection filled the entire screen, then stroked himself vigorously, tugging at it as if he were trying to remove a stubborn root from his garden. He got a full two minutes of film before spurting his viscous semen all over the computer screen, keyboard, and camera. After cleaning off his equipment and washing his hands, Marty watched his video. He was happy with what he saw.

"She'll like that," he muttered to himself. But, deep down, he knew that was unlikely. She'd probably be horrified and disgusted, but that was cool too.

If he'd done any self-analysis, Marty would have been forced to acknowledge the pathetic worm of self-pity and entitlement nestled in his brain that blamed all the women he was too terrified to approach for his loneliness and abstinence. Sending them photos of his penis made him feel empowered, sexually connected to them, whether they wanted that connection or not. If he'd had the requisite empathy and introspection skills, he'd have seen what he was doing amounted to digital rape. But, Marty did not.

He enjoyed visualizing the shocked reactions of the women he sent his photos and videos. He imagined them first appalled, then aroused. Perhaps they would be so impressed with his thick, meaty erection they would stare at it while they masturbated. He knew his eight and a half inches put him comfortably above the average male penis size. Perhaps it wasn't as big as some of the monstrous appendages he'd seen jammed into various orifices in the pornography he watched obsessively, but it was as big or bigger than a lot of them.

Marty often fantasized about the women he digitally assaulted reaching out to him, inviting him over to see it in person, unable to restrain themselves. Maybe even that cashier at the bagel shop down the street with the long black hair, red lipstick, and black eyeshadow and nail polish. The one with breasts larger than his head. He'd jerked off more than once imagining her begging him to put his cock between her massive mammaries. He'd already sent her nearly a dozen photos. When she didn't respond, he began sending her photos of his cock posed next to soda cans and action figures to give an accurate representation of its size. Then videos, like the one he just made.

In response, she'd sent him photos of dead kittens, then other men's penises, some of them severed, and then human corpses. She made a few disparaging remarks about the size of his dick he knew were untrue but hurt nonetheless.

"Why are you sending me kiddie porn? That's a little boy's dick. I'm going to report you for child pornography

He stopped after that comment, not because she had successfully shamed him. Marty knew his cock was bigger than average, probably bigger than any she'd ever had. But he was afraid she'd actually report him to the FBI. He didn't need that in his life.

Marty played the video of him masturbating several times. It was good shit. His cock looked massive. Women should have been falling all over themselves to get a piece of it. But, they largely ignored him. Until this one.

Minutes after he sent her the video, Sheila Alfonso responded.

"I like it. You should bring that piece of meat to me. I want it in my mouth," she replied.

Marty had to read the message several times before he was certain he hadn't misinterpreted it. Then he had to decide whether or not to jack off again right then and there. It might make him less likely to cum prematurely, if she was serious. Of course, it might also make it more difficult to get an erection in the first place. Decisions, decisions.

"Don't you want me?" Sheila added, and Marty realized he'd been so stunned he hadn't responded to her message.

"Of course! Where do you want to meet? Want to come over my place?"

"You come to my place," Sheila replied, then she sent him her address.

Holy shit!

Fear and self-doubt invaded Marty's thoughts. He regarded himself in the mirror above his bureau. His low-hanging gut, skinny arms, sagging pecs, flat, flabby ass, pudgy cheeks, and squinty eyes. He was no fashion model. He knew there were women who found him cute, until he spoke, and his social awkwardness turned them off. He had a habit of not filtering his less enlightened views. Over the years, it had earned him a slap, a drink thrown in his face, and many expressions of disgust. It had also seen him twice called in to HR and forced to take online sensitivity and sexual harassment classes. But Marty thought he could keep his mouth shut, keep his responses to short, one-word answers. He hoped he could. After all, she wanted him for his cock not his wit. He couldn't change his appearance, couldn't lose the extra forty pounds swinging from his gut and butt in the next thirty minutes, but he could work on being charming, or at least, silent.

"Are you coming?"

Shit. He'd zoned out again and forgotten to reply.

"Just getting dressed. I'm on my way," he typed quickly.

Marty spent less than a minute picking out a nice shirt and pants. It was one of five dress shirts and five pairs of pants he owned. One for each day of the work week. He decided on a light blue button-up and grey pants with a brown belt and matching brown shoes. His Monday outfit. Maybe if he folded it nicely, he wouldn't have to rewash it. It all depended on how sweaty he got and whether he'd have time to take a shower before he left Sheila's apartment. He tended to sweat a lot, and he hadn't exerted himself sexually in years. Jerking off to interracial gangbang porn compilations wasn't very aerobic.

It was a thirty-minute drive to Sheila's place. As Marty drove, he went from ecstatic to worried to so self-critical he almost turned the vehicle around and went back home, convinced he would be laughed out of Sheila's apartment, to so overconfident he imagined Sheila dropping to her knees at the sight of his massive cock. The latter dominated his fantasies. Why would she have invited him over if she didn't want the dick? There were photos of him on his social media profile that revealed his face and a few showing his full body. She had to have seen them. He couldn't imagine a woman inviting someone they'd only met online to their apartment without checking their social media profile thoroughly. Unless, of course, she was crazy. But maybe she was the right kind of crazy? Maybe she was just a cock hungry cum-slut who didn't care what his body looked like? He hoped. He really, really hoped.

Sheila's apartment was an old Gothic Victorian building with high gables and ornate wood trim. It had been built sometime around the signing of the Declaration of Independence. Marty half expected there to be a plaque on the front of the building that said "George Washington slept here." A doorman in a crisp black suit and black bow tie was on a cellphone, laughing. A large, bald Black man with a goatee and a laugh that sounded like a demon expressing his joy over the unbaptized babies it was about to consume. He smiled at Marty as he held open the door for him. His smile lasted too long and seemed a bit too amused, as if the two were sharing some joke Marty had somehow missed.

Does he know I'm here to see Sheila? Does she regularly have guys like me over for sex? Maybe this dude has fucked her a few times himself? Marty wondered.

It didn't matter. Marty wasn't looking for a relationship, though it would be nice. If she just used him for sex, kicked him out, and never talked to him again, he was sure he'd get over the heartache.

He walked through the lobby to an antique wooden elevator with glass doors surrounded by an ornate iron cage with intricate designs. The doorman opened the cage, and Marty stepped in. Sheila's apartment was on the top floor. The grinning doorman had to use his keycard on the elevator before he could press the button for the thirteenth floor. Marty had always believed buildings didn't have thirteenth floors.

"The penthouse is private," the doorman explained in answer to a question Marty hadn't asked, then his smile grew noticeably wider. He topped it off with a wink, then stood outside the elevator, staring at Marty, still smiling, while he closed the cage and the elevator doors slowly shut. Once the doors were closed, Marty heard the doorman laugh in that deep, husky, gravely, demonic voice he'd heard when he first arrived at the building. A chill raced the length of Marty's spine. He was suddenly, unreasonably, terrified. He wondered what the guy found so funny.

What don't I know?

There were many possibilities. Is Sheila a transwoman? Marty didn't really care if she was. He occasionally watched "shemale" porn. He knew that wasn't the PC term, but that's what you had to type into the search engines to find it. Maybe she's a call-girl? He wondered. Was she expecting him to pay for this? A trangender call-girl? Was that what the door guy found so hilarious?

As the elevator rose, the possibility he was on his way to see a prostitute solidified in Marty's mind. If she was a prostitute, judging from the building and her penthouse apartment, she was clearly more than he could afford. The doors whooshed open, and Marty stepped out into a small hallway with just a single door at the end of it. It was more of a vestibule than a hallway. The door was seven feet tall and made of black iron with a smoky tinted glass. The design on the door was the image of a demon and an angel cavorting with a dragon. He'd never seen an apartment with an iron door before.

This chick must have some serious money.

He hesitated, standing before the huge door nearly crippled with uncertainty. He took a deep breath, closed his eyes, then knocked. When he opened his eyes, he saw the doorbell. He shook his head and pressed it. Chimes echoed beyond the door like church bells.

The door opened. Two women stood in the doorway. Sheila, looking even more incredible than she did in her photographs, stood wearing a sheer black lace crotchless catsuit. Beside her, in a glossy black latex bodysuit, was the woman from the bagel shop. Her outfit looked like it had been painted on, and her massive breasts appeared even larger than they did in her bagel-shop uniform. Marty's mouth fell open. This was more than a dream come true. This was too good to be true. Even with his cock straining against his boxers for release, warning alarms were going off in Marty's head. Something was wrong. None of this made sense.

"What—what are you doing here?"

"What's wrong? You don't think you can handle both of us?" Sheila said.

"Don't you want me?" The bagel shop girl asked, unzipping her bodysuit until her big beautiful breasts spilled from the latex and hung there, bouncing in the air. Marty's erection threatened to break free from his pants. She reached out and stroked it. All the red flags and alarm bells going off in Marty's head were instantaneously muted.

"Come in," Sheila said.

Marty stumbled forward in a daze. The iron door slammed shut with a loud bang that shook Marty from his stupor. A deep primal instinct within him screamed for him to flee. Terror seeped into his bones. The desire to scream sucked all the moisture from his mouth. Beads of sweat formed on his brow. He began to tremble.

Marty couldn't pinpoint the source of his fear, besides the sheer improbability of the situation. Women like them didn't fuck guys who looked like him after a few dick pics, regardless of what porn would have you believe. This looked, smelled, sounded, and tasted like a trap. Marty felt regret more profound than anything he'd ever experienced. He had the urge to apologize to these women for making them an accomplice in his deviancy. No, victims of it. He had victimized these women. He wanted to cry, certain their husbands or boyfriends were waiting in the next room with baseball bats and lead pipes. He pictured Marsellus Wallace from Pulp Fiction stepping out of hiding with a blowtorch and a pair of pliers.

"I'm gonna get medieval on your ass!"

Despite his fears, the possibility of pussy was too powerful a lure for Marty to walk away despite every cell in his body, every survival instinct in his genetic code, imploring him to. He would feel ridiculous if he began blubbering and crying, apologizing and begging for forgiveness, and they just wanted to fuck. Maybe his fears were another manifestation of his social awkwardness, imagining horrors where none existed.

They took Marty's arms, one on each side, and walked him through the living room. Marty had the feeling he was being carried. He couldn't feel his feet touch the hardwood floors. On one side, Sheila kissed his neck, while on the other, the bagel shop girl unbuttoned his shirt and licked his nipple. Sheila unzipped his pants and freed Marty's cock from his boxer briefs. Both her and the bagel shop girl were stroking his erection in unison. Marty leaned his head back and began to moan, trying his best not to cum. He could not imagine anything worse than ejaculating before he had the chance to fuck these two beauties.

As he was guided into the bedroom, Marty stepped onto the plush carpet and something squished. Then the smell hit him. Rancid meat and blood. His eyes snapped open. He felt his shoes sink into a tacky, dank moistness. He looked down and saw blood oozing up from the carpet. A low moan of helplessness and utter dread escaped him as he looked around.

Bodies. The eviscerated, mutilated, disarticulated bodies of men were strewn haphazardly about the room. At least three different carcasses in various stages of dismemberment. An "X" shaped cross held the arms and torso of a man missing his head and the entire lower half of his body, which Marty was unable to locate. On the bed, another man was strapped down with leather restraints and chains. He'd been castrated, and an incision went from his asshole to beneath his chin. Everything that had been inside him now littered the bed.

The worst of it was on a table in the center of the room. There were bones. Upon a dining table, on silver serving trays sat a human femur, a humerus, and half a ribcage. They'd been gnawed to the bone. The rest of the body lay on the floor beside the cart, similarly vivisected and dismembered. Marty screamed.

He tried to pull away, but the two women had a python-like grip on his arms. Without warning, the kisses on his neck and chest became sharp bites. The stroking of his cock became brutal tugs. Bagel shop girl bit down on his chest and began to thrash like a Pitbull playing tug-of-war. Marty's screams grew more shrill. He tried to push her off of him. Sheila bit down on the side of his neck and jerked her head sharply, ripping stringy meat and blubbery, popcorn-colored fat from right beneath his jaw. Blood spurted from his lacerated carotid, coating her face in a grisly red bukkake. She still had a grip on his cock, as did the bagel shop girl. They twisted and pulled his sex in opposite directions while clawing his scrotum with their long, manicured nails, ripping it open as if trying to release a newborn from the amniotic sac. His testes spilled from his torn nutsack, dangling on thin spermatic cords and testicular ligaments like tiny bungee jumpers. Marty's scream reached a pitch he was sure would shatter windows. His throat felt raw and burned as if he'd swallowed ash.

He looked at the two women, expecting to find they'd transformed into demons or vampires, but they were still just two ridiculously sexy women who happened to have a torture room in their penthouse decorated with dismembered corpses. The bagel-shop girl ripped a sizeable chunk from his chest the size of a child's fist. Sheila knelt between his legs. Marty's cock shriveled in full retreat. He had a moment of embarrassment at being seen in such a diminished state, then his horror returned as she plopped one of his exposed testes into her mouth and bit down on it, crushing it like a grape. The pain doubled him over. He watched her slowly chew; blood, semen, and saliva drooled down her face. She reached out for the next one, plopping that one in her mouth too. With his free hand, Marty punched her, splitting her lip and causing her to bite down. He screamed again.

The bagel shop girl now had his flaccid, shriveled cock in her mouth. Marty whimpered and began to ugly cry. Tears, snot, and saliva hung from his chin in long ropes as he sobbed.

"Please. Please, don't. I'm so sorry. I know it was wrong. I shouldn't have sent those photos. I shouldn't have. Just let me go. I promise, I'll never do it again. Don't bite my dick off. Please don't bite it off!" Before waiting for an answer, he punched Sheila again; she fell back, his testicle still in her mouth, stretching the cords and ligaments like rubber bands until they popped. Marty nearly vomited as agony churned his intestines into tight knots. She fell on her ass and just stared at him, smiling as she slowly chewed. He had broken her nose, but the crazy bitch didn't seem to mind. He felt another terrible pain and realized he'd somehow forgotten about bagel shop girl's mouth around his cock. She had bitten down with her blunt little teeth and was tugging hard, trying to tear it off. He grabbed her by the head, trying his damnedest to pry her teeth from his cock.

"Please! Please don't bite it off!"

Marty had two beautiful women, one with his balls in her mouth, the other with his cock halfway down her throat. He'd watched countless hours of internet porn featuring the same scenario. He never imagined it could be so fucking horrible. She tore his cock off, ripping it from its moorings with a sound like unspooling duct tape. Marty fell onto the blood-drenched carpet shrieking like a scalded infant. A red fountain spewed from the avulsion between his legs where his penis had been. Sheila finished eating his balls, and was now sharing his cock with the girl from the bagel shop. Her mouth was on the ragged end while the head was still in the bagel shop girl's mouth. It was actually pretty hot, in a grisly, disturbing way. Marty felt that familiar stirring, and realized it was just a phantom sensation. His dick wasn't there anymore. He began to laugh despite the terrific agony he was in.

The two women turned and looked at him.

"What the fuck are you laughing at?"

Marty knew he would be dead soon. They would torture him, cut him up, and eat him like they'd done the others. He bet that rich bitch, Sheila, had enough money to make all their bodies disappear. The doorman would probably help. Marty would be just another missing person. He continued to laugh.

"What's so fucking funny?" Sheila asked. She stood, hands on her hips, a piece of Marty's cock flesh dangled from her mouth as she chewed absentmindedly.

"I knew you bitches wanted my cock!" Marty said, as he was overcome by another fit of laughter.

He would be screaming again soon.

Chapter Nine

BLOOD-SOAKED SAVIOR

He breathed so deeply
of the pestilence in the air
smiling like a jack-o-lantern
a jack-ass sneering leering smile

That is how I knew
He did not value his life
That is how I knew
he'd embrace oblivion
He already had

The death I offered
would be quicker than drowning
like Elizabeth drowned
Slowly suffocating
smothered by her own lungs
over days and weeks

The death I offered
would be quicker
than your loved ones

standing helplessly
at your deathbed
like I stood at Elizabeth's
watching her gasp and wheeze
eyes full of terror and pain
begging me to take the pain away

I could take hours
take my sweet precious time
and still be more merciful
than disease
An angel of mercy
A blood-soaked savior

I read all his posts
refusing to live in fear
to cover his smug face
to keep six feet
from moist air
aerosolized droplets
of smothering
suffocating
coughing
wheezing
choking
organ failing
finality

That is how I knew
He did not value his life
that he'd embrace oblivion
like a coveted lover
an expensive whore
wearing pox like trophies
plague like jewelry
The death I offered

would be more merciful

even if I took hours

He walked around the store
Face bare
unmasked
like the selfish people
who infected my Elizabeth
Exhaling death
wheezing
coughing
choking
smothering
death
as she'd waited on their tables
Because we couldn't afford
I could not afford
for her to quarantine
for her to stay home safe
And men like him
breathed death into her lungs
coughing
wheezing
choking
organ failing
fatality

His arrogance surrounded him
a noxious cloud
of moist air
aerosolized disease
And he breathed deep
of the pestilence around him

I watched him shop

Watched him argue with tellers
refusing to cover his face
like the customers who killed Elizabeth
breathed death into her lungs
wheezing
coughing
choking
smothering
death

"This is goddamn America!"

He bellowed
at the teller who asked him
to put on a mask

"It's a free country!"

He shrieked
at the customer who came to her defense
A geyser of nonsense

"She's just doing her job."

"There's a pandemic."

"People are dying!"

He didn't care
He refused
to live in fear

That's how I knew
I knew
I knew
he would welcome me

like a blood-soaked savior

I followed him out
into a barren night
A quiet night
A moonless
soundless
careless
cautionless
night

I followed him to his truck
festooned with flags
Black and white and blue flags
Trumped with stickers
and slogans
"Come and take it!"
"Four more years!"
"Fuck Biden!"
"Make America Great Again!"
Again?
Again?
Again?
A geyser of nonsense

I would make him a martyr
for his hopeless cause

I wore my mask
I wore my gloves
I closed the distance

I struck his stubborn head
with a rock
I kicked his hateful mouth
with a working man's boot

Dusty and mud-crusted
A working man's boot
I couldn't find my hammer
I hadn't planned for this

I watched his eyes roll back
his arms flail
His mouth
His head
Red
Red
Red

My t-shirt turned red
Head wounds bleed like lies
and dogma
from the mouths of the ignorant
a geyser of nonsense

I wrapped his head
in my favorite t-shirt
my Star Wars t-shirt
that wasn't red before
and a grocery bag
that wasn't red before

I bound his limbs
with extension cords
bungee cords
a two-foot piece of twine
whatever I had in my trunk
I hadn't planned for this

I hadn't planned to silence
that geyser of nonsense

I put him in my trunk
I put his groceries in my trunk
I kept my mask on
I kept my gloves on
But,
I didn't keep my distance

I took him to the basement
laid him on the table
where my Elizabeth
used to do her crafts
scrapbooking
knitting
needlepoint
sewing masks
for essential workers
like her
because it was essential
that assholes
got their greasy burgers
and overpriced milkshakes
more essential
than Elizabeth's life

I wiped away tears
as I tied him to the table
with bungee cords
and twine
and strips of fabric
and duct tape
whatever I could find
In Elizabeth's craft box

I wiped away tears
When I found
her orange-handled scissors

the twenty-dollar scissors
Elizabeth's craft scissors
The one's we'd argued about

"Why did anyone need twenty-dollar scissors?"

I needed them now

The man without the mask
squirmed and screamed
wailed and wiggled
And I reassured him
His death would be quick
Quicker than Elizabeth's
Quicker than the
wheezing
coughing
choking
smothering
death
awaiting him
If I hadn't saved him

I would make sure
he only suffered for hours
Not weeks
Not like Elizabeth

I would make sure
his loved ones
would never stand helpless
by his deathbed
watching him gasp and wheeze

I would save him
I would save him

The first hour
I removed his smug smirk
ripping off his cheeks
and lips
like peeling a mango
wet, sticky, juicy, bloody
dripping from my fingers
And made him smile

The second hour
his smile disturbed me
annoyed me
angered me
smiling like a jack-o-lantern
a jack-ass sneering leering smile
Elizabeth hadn't been smiling
neither should he
So, I removed his teeth
dug them out
one by one
with Elizabeth's scissors
And knitting needles
It took work
messy bloody work
But it was better than Elizabeth's death
It was a mercy

The death I offered
would be quicker than drowning
like Elizabeth drowned
Slowly suffocating
smothered by her own lungs
over days and weeks

I could take hours
take my sweet precious time

And still be more merciful
than disease
An angel of mercy
A blood-soaked savior

The third hour
I made sure
he would never reproduce
he will never reproduce

The fourth hour
The last hour
I used those twenty-dollar scissors
And a claw hammer
cracked open his sternum
and removed his gray and black lungs
like removing a fetus from the womb
A cardiovascular cesarean
carbon-stained
nicotine-saturated
cancerous
lungs
It took work to get them out
messy
bloody work

He screamed
and wailed
and shrieked
against the gag
of duct-tape and fabric scraps
as I pulled
and tugged
and cut out his lungs
with the orange-handled
twenty-dollar scissors

He thrashed
convulsed
fought
and failed
and wheezed
and gurgled
and suffocated
drowned
and died
much faster than
Elizabeth had

I was his blood-soaked savior
he hadn't suffered
like Elizabeth suffered
Oh, he suffered
but not like Elizabeth had
And he kept his freedom
And his rights
to a bare face
but not to breathe
not to exhale
moist air
a noxious cloud
of aerosolized disease
to be inhaled
by essential workers
risking death
to bring him a fucking burger
But not to breathe
not to breathe
ever
ever

Again
And no one

No one
No one
would ever tell him
to wear a goddamn mask

"This is goddamn America!"

I wiped away tears

Goddamn America.

Chapter Ten

BLUE & RED

They ran. Mathew was looking back, turning around and firing his shotgun at the mutated things racing after them while trying his best not to trip over some trash in the road or his own feet. Rashad's weapon was still in its holster. He was just hauling ass, not bothering to try to shoot them. He looked over at Mathew and frowned, rolling his eyes and shaking his head like he was looking at the world's biggest fool. Mathew hated when Rashad looked at him like that.

"You're just wasting ammo. You ain't hittin' shit! Just keep running!" Rashsad shouted.

"I'm trying to slow them down!"

"By shooting all over the damn place! You ain't even aiming! Just fucking run!"

The things didn't have much stamina. Rashad had killed a few in the past just by running them to death. One at a time, they'd collapsed of heart attacks after just a few blocks. The other thing that gave Rashad and Mathew hope was that the things were weak, flabby, and slow. They tended to have big, fat, low-hanging bellies, and skinny arms, blinking, twitching, and sniffing. They were mostly scavengers, carrion eaters, scarfing down garbage like giant raccoons. But, when there was live prey available, they turned carnivorous, hunting in large packs to overwhelm and bring down their outnumbered prey. One on one, either one of them could have beaten one of those things to death with their bare hands. It was only in huge mobs, like the one currently chasing them, that they were really dangerous.

Mathew hated running. It made him feel like a coward. Besides, all the muscle he was carrying made him only slightly faster than the creatures chasing him. He wondered how many of those things he could take out before they got him. He had the shotgun, and he had some martial arts training, and he was pretty muscular. He was pretty sure he could take out six or seven of them. Rashad could probably take out another four or five with his Beretta. That still left almost a dozen. Terrible odds. Rashad was right. It was better for them to try to outrun them.

"I am so fucking sick of this fucked up world!"

"Just keep running. I'll scrounge you up a beer once we're safe."

"Fuck the beer. I'm gonna find me a bottle of Wild Turkey!"

*

Earlier that day ...

Rashad pulled a new Bic Quatro from the pack, sprayed Brut shaving foam into his hand and smeared it onto his face. Slowly and carefully, he shaved around his mouth, chin, and jawline. All it would take was a little bit of hair between his face and the gas mask and it wouldn't fit properly and might allow whatever biological or chemical weapons were still in the air to infiltrate his lungs. He'd been lucky so far. He had no idea why he was still alive, but he was grateful for it and had no intention of giving up the gift of life over some careless mistake.

The clean room was airtight. The only air that came in

from the outside had to go through seven air filters. Fresh oxygen had to be pumped in continually, and they were starting to run out. They had to get more. The only oxygen tank they knew of was three miles away, and they would have to cart seven or eight containers with them in order to bring back enough oxygen to last another week.

"Hurry the fuck up, white boy!"

"Fuck you, jiggaboo! I'm moving as fast as I can. "

"You'd better kill all that jiggaboo shit, peckerwood. You don't know me like that."

"Then you kill all that peckerwood and cracker shit."

"I didn't call you no cracker."

"Not today you didn't, but you have."

Mathew walked out of the bathroom wearing a hazmat suit with just the pants on. The top half of the suit was bunched up around his waist. His large muscles glistened with sweat.

"What the fuck do you work out so hard for? Ain't no more bitches to impress, and I damn sure don't think your cracker ass is sexy."

"It's for them mutant motherfuckers out there, spook. I'm stayin' in shape so I stay off their fuckin' menu."

"I told you to watch that spook shit!" Rashad yelled, jumping up and grabbing his gun, a 9mm Beretta. Rashad was not a small man. He was six-four and nearly three hundred pounds. Ten years ago, he'd been a college running back with dreams of the NFL. Two years ago, he was a computer repair technician working in the clean room at Texas Computer Surgeons repairing damaged hard drives. Then that idiot president decided to nuke North Korea and the entire world had gone to hell. In a matter of weeks, everyone he knew was dead except Mathew.

He pointed the gun at Mathew's head. Mathew's shotgun was on the other side of the room. He'd be dead before he could reach it.

"Take that shit back, white boy!"

"Nigga, you called me a cracker!"

"Now you just called me a nigga! What the fuck is wrong with you?"

"I said it with an "a" at the end, though."

"That don't fuckin' matter!"

"Man, get that gun out my face before I make you eat that mutherfucker. We're running out of oxygen again. I ain't tryin to use up all of mine fightin' with your fat ass."

Mathew was a college wrestler with dreams of becoming a cage fighter. His daddy had been a congressman or a senator or something before the bombs and the chemical and biological weapons and the radioactivity and the damn mutants.

"You can't fight, white boy. The only fight you ever had you got your ass kicked."

"I was eight!"

"See, if you could fight worth a damn, you'd have had more fights. I fought all the time in high school and college. I kicked more ass than you ever dreamed about kickin'."

"You beat up mutherfuckers smaller than you. That ain't fightin'. I was trainin' to fight other fighters. That takes real heart."

"You don't know shit."

"You don't know shit, mutherfucker! Now get that fuckin' gun out my face!"

"After you apologize."

"We're runnin' out of air fuckin' around!"

"Then fuckin' apologize!"

"I apologize, mutherfucker. Damn!"

"Thank you," Rashad said, tucking the Beretta back into his shoulder holster.

"I'm gonna whoop your fat black ass one of these days."

"If you ever thought about tryin' to whoop my ass, I'd end up being the last man on earth."

Mathew had been a client of Rashad's. He was in the office raving about some papers he needed for his plumbing business that were on his computer when it crashed and how he needed it ASAP. Rashad was explaining to him that if he didn't have so many viruses on his computer from all the internet porn sites he visited, his hard drive wouldn't have crashed. They had both fallen silent when news of the global holocaust began coming in. They were lucky because the clean room they used at Texas Computer Surgeons not only filtered outside air using a system of HEPA filters, but the outside air could be shut off entirely and fresh oxygen pumped in. The room itself was kept at positive pressure so that when staff entered or exited through the airlocks or if there was ever a leak, air would leak out of the chamber rather than allowing unfiltered air to leak in.

They had an air shower that blasted any dust, contaminants, or pollutants from their clothes before they entered the airlock and put on their protective gear, gas masks, gloves, hats, and shoe covers. It was the perfect environment to help them survive the radioactive chemical cloud that rolled across America, killing everything it touched. As soon as he heard about the cloud on the little radio he kept on his desk tuned to National Public Radio and saw that it was headed right for them, Rashad rushed inside the clean room and barricaded himself inside. Unfortunately, not before Mathew leapt the counter and charged in behind him. They had been there ever since, exiting only to get food and water, gas for the power generator, and more oxygen for the tanks.

At first, Rashad had been happy he wasn't alone. Mathew helped carry water, gas, and other supplies that would have been difficult for him to manage alone. Then they started talking politics, specifically, who was to blame for the end of the world. He had been shocked to discover that his conservative roommate blamed liberals for the downfall of civilization even though it had been a conservative president who ordered the preemptive strike.

"If the Democrats hadn't cut the defense budget, those damn terrorists wouldn't have attacked us and we wouldn't have had to blast their asses."

"And how many damn bombs do you think we needed? We had enough to end the world a hundred times over."

"Yeah, but when we started reducing our nuclear stockpile, it was a sign of weakness. That's why North Korea attacked us."

Rashad shook his head.

"They didn't attack us, you fucking idiot. We attacked them! We fired the first nukes at them!"

"But that's only because they were building their own nukes and chemical and biological weapons and shit. We had to strike first. They would have never tried that shit when Reagan was in office."

"Reagan? You've got to be fucking kidding me. Why do all you white conservative mutherfuckers idolize that old fool so much? Do you know what his bullshit 'trickle-down' economic theory did to the poor people in America? Do you even know what the ghettoes were like in the eighties? He's the one that started shipping cocaine into this country, using the CIA to flood the ghettoes with it. He turned the young black male into public enemy number one at a time when we should have been on the rise. His bitch ass set black folks back about twenty years in this country. He set race relations between blacks and whites back thirty years. And, he increased the gap between the rich and the poor about a hundredfold."

"That's just a bunch of black militant conspiracy bullshit. What are you, an Obama-lover?"

"A what? Is that some kind of sneaky way to say nigger-lover, you piece of shit?"

"If his weak ass had struck back in twenty twelve, we wouldn't be in this mess now. We could have blown them off the map before they ever built all those damn weapons. Instead, he talked to them, like he could stop them with his teletype speeches."

"And how do you know they didn't have biological weapons back then?"

"They didn't."

"How do you know?"

"Because I know. That black bastard ruined this country!"

"Bullshit! That white piece of shit who fired the missiles ruined this country along with the rest of the world. How do we know they ever would have used those weapons if we hadn't fired first?"

"Who builds a weapon of mass destruction without the intention of using it?"

"And that's what the rest of the world thought about us with all of our nukes. That's why they armed themselves with their own weapons. That's why we needed to disarm."

"Nah, those nukes were the only things keeping those gooks in check. But, of course you'd side with the terrorists, being a Muslim and all."

"I ain't no damn Muslim! I'm an atheist."

"Yeah, but you're a Muslim atheist ain't you? How else did you get a Muslim name like Rashad? You one of them followers of Farrakhan ain't you?"

"A Muslim atheist? That don't even make no damn sense! And Rashad ain't just a Muslim name, it's an African American name. And I ain't no Muslim."

"Whatever, man. You still sympathize with them."

"With who? There ain't nobody left! There ain't no more terrorists! There ain't no more Nation of Islam! There ain't no more America! We're all that's left!"

Mathew rolled up the sleeve of his hazmat suit to reveal a tattoo of the United States flag next to an orange Longhorns tattoo and a Confederate flag.

"As long as my white ass is alive and breathing, America is alive."

Rashad rolled his eyes and turned his back on the man.

"That's about the dumbest shit I ever saw. All you rednecks waving a Confederate flag with one arm and the US flag with the other. The South rebelled against our country, you know? They tried to secede from the United States. They were a bunch of fucking traitors, and you stupid mother-fuckers fly both flags. What's next? Swastikas?"

"It ain't the same. The Confederate flag celebrates our heritage. Nazis were the enemy."

Rashad shrugged. "The South was the enemy too. They were fighting against America."

"You just–you just don't understand."

Rashad nodded, a sly grin on his face.

"You know I'm right. You flying an enemy flag on your arm, traitor."

"Fuck you, ya black bastard!"

Rashad laughed and shook his head.

"Yeah, but I'm a black bastard who knows better than to wear a traitor's flag on my arm," Rashad said.

Mathew looked at his arm, then tugged his sleeve back down.

"You don't know what the fuck you're talking about."

"Yeah, you know I'm right."

"Fuck you, darkie!"

"Cracker!"

"Nigg–"

"Go ahead. Say it. I swear it'll be the last word you ever speak," Rashad said, placing a hand on the Beretta.

Mathew looked down at the gun. He had his shotgun slung over his shoulder now. He was pretty sure he could pull it around and get off a shot before Rashad could. And he didn't need to be as accurate. But then he'd be alone. Just him and those things. As much as Rashad got on his nerves, it was better than being all by himself in a world full of monsters.

"All you people do is shoot each other."

Rashad scoffed.

"I don't know why you hate brothas so much, with that thick-ass country accent, you sound just like a hoodrat."

"I don't talk like ya'll."

Rashad snickered.

"Yeah, okay."

They finished putting on all of their personal protection equipment and stepped into the airlock together.

"Why the hell couldn't I have gotten locked in that clean room with Halle Barry or Gianna Micheals or somebody instead of some dumb redneck? This sucks."

"Because Halle Barry can't kick mutant ass the way I can."

Rashad paused in deep thought as they exited the clean room and walked out into the lobby.

"Mutants? You really think those things used to be human?"

"What else could they be?"

"I don't know. Aliens. Demons. Republicans."

Mathew laughed this time.

"You just don't quit, do ya, boy?"

"I'm gonna let that boy shit slide this time, but only because I don't have the time to be fightin' wit' you."

"Oh, lighten up. I'm just bustin' your balls. Now, help me move these barricades."

They had parked trucks in front of each entrance to the building. That only left windows as entrances and exits, and all the windows were made of tempered glass coated with plastic an inch thick for sound and security. A bullet couldn't get through them. But there was one small window they'd managed to hack through with an axe, creating an opening just big enough for them to squeeze through. They had parked a large golf cart, which used to be used by security to patrol the building, in front of the opening. To get out, they had to slide the thing over. They kept the brake on to make it hard to move. Whenever they needed to move it, they just disengaged the brake and then they could roll it fairly easily.

Their SUV, a big yellow Hummer, was parked on the other side. The two of them climbed through the window, and in two steps, they were in the vehicle. More guns and ammunition were stored in a locked box in the back of the Hummer, just in case they ever got surrounded and needed to fight their way out. It hadn't happened yet, though. Whatever the creatures were that had taken over the earth, they didn't work well in packs. They came at you one by one, which made it easier to fight them off ... so far.

"Well, shall we?"

"Drive, motherfucker! What, do you need permission?"

Mathew started up the Hummer, and they headed down the street, weaving between the rusted husks of vehicles whose owners were long dead—or mutated.

"I hope we don't see any of those things. They freak me the fuck out. They kind of look like him."

"What? You're crazy."

"I mean, they're orange! Isn't that kind of a weird coincidence?"

"They ain't orange. They're red. They're some kinda demons. Now that there ain't no more people, hell must've gotten overrun, busted its seams or some shit."

"Man, that's a damn movie!"

"What movie?"

"Night of The Living Dead. When there's no more room in hell, the dead will walk the earth. Or something like that. And these ain't zombies. They're mutants."

"Whatever. My point is, it ain't got nothing to do with him."

"Except that he started it all. He fired the first shot. What if ... I mean what if those chemical weapons didn't come from North Korea? What if they were ours? What if they came from right here in America? Some shit the Idiot-In-Chief came up with to make everyone look like him?"

"Like the Joker's laughing gas that turns people's skin white? Now who's tripping? You're getting theories from a comic book."

"Or ... he got his inspiration from one."

"They ain't orange!"

They turned the corner, and the street ahead was clogged with the things. Thirty or forty of them with orange peel complexions and popcorn-colored hair, lumbering around outside of an old hamburger franchise, stuffing their mouths with moldy, rotting, irradiated meat and fries. They turned in unison and began running toward the Hummer.

"Shit!"

"See! See! I told you those fucking things were orange!"

"Really? This ain't the fucking time for I told you so!"

"Before I fucking die, I want to hear you admit that I was right."

"We ain't gonna die, boy. I'll run those fucking things the fuck over!"

"No! Back up! Put it in reverse! You go barreling into them and we'll get stuck and then surrounded."

Rashad reached for the steering wheel, but Mathew shoved him back. They fought for a moment, but when Mathew stomped down on the accelerator, Rashad relented. He didn't want to be the reason they crashed the Hummer and got them both eaten alive. He braced for impact as the Hummer raced into the crowd of Cheeto-colored mutants.

The things didn't even get out of the way. Instead, they raced directly at the Hummer, slamming into it with pathetic little thumps that barely left a dent in the Hummer's grille. The Hummer crushed more than a dozen of them before broken and splintered bone ruptured their tires and a river of gore clogged up the engine. The Hummer didn't even roll. It just stopped.

"Fuck! I guess we have no choice but to fight now, you fucking asshole!"

Rashad had a pistol in each hand as he kicked open the door of the SUV and leapt out, firing into the surging crowd of orange and yellow. Mathew grabbed the shotgun, slung a bandolier of shells over his shoulder, and started firing. A particularly soft and doughy one ran awkwardly forward, slipping and sliding in the blood and entrails of its pulverized fellow freaks. It fell at Mathew's feet before it could reach him, and Mathew bashed its skull open with the butt of the shotgun, then lifted the gun and fired two rounds into two others before pausing to reload. They were coming too quickly.

"Run! Fucking run, you idiot!"

"Don't call me a fucking idiot!" Mathew yelled back, but Rashad had already taken off down the street.

"Shit. Wait for me, you son-of-a-bitch!"

"Fuck that! You catch up!"

The slack-jawed, cheddar cheese-complexioned mutants gave chase, tripping and stumbling over each other, making sniffing noises and seeming to leer obscenely at Mathew and Rashad like they were two porn stars in a Vegas hotel room. Mathew started running.

"Come on!" Rashad yelled, still several yards ahead of Mathew, though the big man was doing his best Usain Bolt impersonation, trying to close the distance between himself and his unlikely roommate.

They finally put enough distance between themselves and the mob of mutants that they could slow down to catch their breath and pick off the few creatures who'd almost managed to catch them.

After a few deep breaths, they started moving again. Not running, just walking briskly. They turned another corner and skidded to a halt. There, in the middle of the street, stood a familiar face. It was one of the mutants. This one wore an ill-fitting, baggy blue suit, a thick red tie that hung past his bloated waistline, and a red "Make America Great Again" baseball cap.

"Oh, you have got to be fucking kidding me!"

"I fucking told you! I told you! Still happy you voted for him? Why don't you go over there and take a selfie with him? Get his fucking autograph."

"Okay, okay. You made your fucking point. This doesn't prove anything."

"No. But this is damn sure going to feel good!"

Rashad took the shotgun from Mathew, slid a couple

shells from the big guy's bandolier, and loaded them. The slobbering, sniffling, mutant thing wobbled forward, jowls and chins wagging beneath its pumpkin face as it charged. Rashad stepped forward and shoved the shotgun directly into the creature's face and pulled the trigger, splattering the top of the thing's skull and the minute contents of its skull all over the asphalt.

"You've been impeached, motherfucker!"

"Feel better now?"

"Yeah, a little."

"I still wouldn't vote for Hillary."

Rashad just shook his head.

"No wonder this world went to shit. We got exactly what we deserved."

Chapter Eleven

PUNK ROCK REVENGE PORN

I hated the taste
of sweat, cigarettes, and beer
'til I tasted it
on that violent winter night
when we shared a kiss

Miranda's dyed red hair
pale skin
a gaudy tapestry
of morbid tattoos
Skulls
Demons
Vampires
Ravens and tombstones
Verses from
Edgar Allen Poe
Charles Baudelaire
And Comte de Lautreamont
Lyrics from Depeche Mode
The Cure
and Skinny Puppy

I read her like a chapbook
As I undressed her
Kissed a Depeche Mode lyric
Giving in to sin
Making my fucked up life
livable

We shared secrets that night
huddled in our spiked leather jackets
In the stygian shadows
of an abandoned
dilapidated
bicentennial bank

I told her
about the girl who broke my heart
while she sucked my cock
And I spilled angry
unselfconscious
cathartic tears
and squeezed her throat
fucked her throat
'til she wept
liquid shadows
of black mascara

Miranda told me
about the father
who took
her innocence
while she freed her breast
from torn black lace
and fed me her nipple

We made promises
as we fucked

on cold concrete
in stygian shadows
Shadows
fucking ecstatically
within shadows

I made her a promise
to fuck her in her father's blood
as I kissed
my way
down a Baudelaire poem
from Le Fluers de Mal

"My youth was nothing
but dark storms
pierced here and there
by beams of sunlight"

I wanted to be
her beam of sunlight
I thought
tasting the coppery tang
of menstrual blood
as I licked her to orgasm

She promised to be
my avenging angel
my valkyrie
My Bonnie
As she guided me inside
the sweet
moist
heat
at the center of her

We whispered

about slit throats
castration
and mastectomy
skull fucking
and cock and ball torture
as we rutted like beasts
like demons
sweat-soaked angels
fueled by hormones
angst and fury
scraping our knees and backs
on concrete
cold
as unforgiving hearts

We whispered
about the sensuous sound
of their screams
of their begging
of their regret
of their wheezing
rattling
gurgling
death
her pussy clenched me
as she climaxed again

She wrapped her legs tight
Around my hips
not allowing me to pull out
as I roared
cursed God
and came inside her
No birth control
No condom
No HIV test

1988
The middle of the AIDS crisis
This was a trust fall
a blood pact
a commitment
deeper than a pinky swear

The sun rose
We shrank from it
like evil things
that only flourished
in darkness
Murder pacts
sealed in semen
and menstrual blood

We took the L train
huddled against each other
hiding our dour faces
from the rush hour commuters
in each other's
spiked black leather jackets

A middle-aged woman
in nurse's scrubs
scowled and shook her head
while Miranda stroked my switchblade
through my black leather pants
and I licked the axe blade
concealed beneath her jacket

"This is her stop"
I said
not meaning Miranda
but the girl who broke my heart
the girl who owed me

a heart

We skipped off the train
wincing
against the pale December sun
like evil things
that only flourished
in darkness
Murder pacts
sealed in semen
and menstrual blood

We skipped down the road
to Chrissy's house
giving in to sin
to make my fucked up life
livable

We will take back
all the love she wasted
take back those lonely hours
take back the lies and betrayals
Miranda whispered
while she stroked my switchblade
through my black leather pants

Miranda knocked on Chrissy's door
then knocked on Chrissy's skull
with an axe blade

"Take off her clothes."
Miranda said
after we dragged Chrissy inside

She laid on the carpet
arms spread

like Jesus on the cross
A halo of red roses
encrusting her head
roses that dripped
and splattered
and spread across the carpet

I removed her shorts and shirt
"She does have perfect tits,"
Miranda said.
"They are beautiful, " I whispered
remembering the taste and feel of them

"Want 'em?" Miranda asked. "Souvenirs?"

I nodded
of course I wanted them
I wanted her tits
her ass
her pussy
her lips
her heart
all the love she'd thrown away
all those lonely hours
all the lies and betrayals
all the tears of self-loathing

Miranda
took
her
apart
Gave her to me
piece by piece
Souvenirs
giving in
to sin

We left with a doggy bag
filled with bloody memories
Left to catch the L train
to Miranda's house
left Chrissy
spread out like Jesus
on her living room floor
surrounded by roses
that dripped
and splattered
and spread across the carpet

I pushed Miranda's doorbell
the door to her parent's house
I pushed the switchblade
between her father's ribs
When he answered the door

I could feel his heartbeat
Vibrate the blade
Feel each beat
In my fingers
In the palm of my hand
Miranda's father's life
In the palm of my hand
Miranda's father's heart
In my fingers
Miranda
in the palm
of my hand
A trust fall
a blood pact
a commitment
deeper than a pinky swear
and Miranda stroked the switchblade
in her father's heart

We spent the afternoon
cutting
chopping
amputating
castrating
disemboweling
and fucking
in Miranda's father's blood

Shadows
fucking ecstatically
within shadows
dark storms
pierced here and there
by beams of sunlight
Giving in to sin
Making our fucked up lives
livable

Chapter Twelve

THE BLISS POINT

"Some of you are not going to like what I have to say," James said as he paced back and forth behind the pulpit, possessed by an abundance of energy and enthusiasm, a religious fervor that filled his eyes with fire and his every motion with manic vitality. He was filled with the spirit, the Holy Spirit.

"You'll call me a blasphemer, a pervert. Say I am promoting sin. And I agree with you on the latter. I am promoting sin. Sin for the glory of our Lord and Savior, Jesus Christ! But I cannot agree with you on the former. I am no pervert. Obeying our natural instincts and desires is not perversion. Denying them. That is the perversion."

He wore a simple white shirt buttoned all the way to the top. A black sports coat and black pants. His head was shaved, and there was a crucifix tattooed on his left temple. James had a tribal tattoo on his chin that made him appear to have a goatee, but he had no facial hair. He looked more like a biker or a punk rocker than a preacher. His blue/ green eyes sparkled like stars.

Reverend Doctor James Watson's storefront congregation was small but enthusiastic. It had begun in his apartment as a bible study for those who felt unwelcome in the church, liberals, those with alternative lifestyles, homosexuals, the promiscuous, those who questioned, and those who didn't believe in turning the other cheek. James was a psychiatrist who'd specialized in alternative sexuality, and he'd spent years counseling men and women wracked with guilt over the way they were wired, trying desperately to change, to conform to what the world considered normal. Homosexuals trying to turn straight. Sadists and masochists trying to live vanilla lives. Transexuals, adult babies, human puppies and kittens, every deviation imaginable from what religion and society arbitrarily judged normal. Many of them had been shunned by their families and churches and wanted desperately to find a place where they could be accepted, so James had given them that. He opened his home to them and welcomed them in.

Word spread of his doctrine of acceptance, and his study group quickly outgrew his one-bedroom apartment. So, he'd rented space in what was a swinger's club in the evenings, and with the help of a couple dozen volunteers, he'd transformed it into a real church.

Today, there were quite a few new faces. He recognized less than half the congregation, but James knew better than to be overly optimistic. Few of them would remain for the entire sermon. Fewer still would ever come back. He was well aware of how radical his message was. It was no accident he'd built his church in a swinger's club. Many of his new congregants were swingers who'd stumbled in during the day, expecting an orgy, and stayed for the sermon, enthralled by James' words of salvation, just as he had hoped. Now, they returned every Sunday, wishing to receive absolution for their sins, to rid themselves of guilt after an evening of debauchery. They weren't the ones who usually stormed out of his little parish accusing him of heresy. It was the walk-ins, spill-over from other congregations in the neighborhood who came in without a clue. He learned long ago to use their outrage as a teaching moment for his flock.

James held up the bible, closing his eyes and bowing his head as he continued. He knocked on the bible with his free hand.

"I know this runs counter to everything you ever learned in church, but it isn't counter to this. It is all in line with Jesus's teachings. That's right. You have been told to avoid sin, to deny your animal instincts, the very urges and impulses authored by the creator. But I say that you know the creator by his creations, by his works. And when you look at those animals so programmed that they cannot disobey their instincts, what do you see?"

There were a few confused looks from the newcomers. His regulars smiled knowingly. One of them called out: "Sin!" James smiled and pointed to the voluptuous middle-aged woman in the front row who was dressed inappropriately for any church but this one, in a transparent sheer dress through which her black lace panties, bra, and garter were completely visible.

"That's right, sister! You see every act that mankind has determined to be sinful. And don't be fooled, it is man and not God who has proclaimed it so. You see homosexuality. You see promiscuity. You see polyamory and adultery. You see rape and sodomy. You see theft. You see greed, lust, envy, wrath, and deceit. You even see murder, all throughout nature. And you have all tried to resist these primal urges. And you have all failed. Each and every one of you has failed. No human being in the history of mankind has resisted these urges. Not Mother Teressa, not Ghandi, not Dr. Martin Luther King Jr., no one. They have all sinned at some point in their lives. Because what you are attempting isn't possible! It isn't. It is not possible to live without sin, because God has preprogrammed you to be sinners. We are born in sin!"

"Amen!" a man shouted from the back of the room, ripping off his clothes and diving onto the woman next to him, who was already peeling herself out of her skin-tight red dress. The two of them began furiously fucking in the aisle.

An overweight woman who had come with her thin, balding
husband and two obese kids, stood abruptly, knocking over
metal folding chairs as she hustled them up the aisle and out
of the church.

"You are all crazy, and you're all going to hell!" she yelled
pointing an accusatory finger at James.

"We're going to hell?" James chuckled. "No, I don't think
so. Do you know the ONLY way, according to the bible, that
you can go to hell now, after Jesus's sacrifice? That is to deny
Jesus Christ as your Lord and Savior. Anyone here deny the
divinity of Jesus Christ?"

"No!" the congregation replied in unison.

"Anyone here not accept the love of Christ into your
hearts?"

"No!" they all replied once again.

"So then how do you think a sin, or even a multitude of
sins, would damn you to hell if Jesus died for your sins? How
can anyone be damned who accepts Jesus Christ as their Lord
and savior when he himself proclaimed that you were saved?
That through him you would not die, but have eternal life,
that you would sit beside him and his father, our God, in
heaven? Jesus died in the knowledge that mankind was helpless before sin, unable to resist the instinctual drive to sin,
because we are all, at our core, at our essence, at our primal
nature, sinners. Now, how is it possible for a born sinner to
deny his or her very identity? Can a fish not swim? An eagle
refuse to soar? And Jesus knew that you could not live
without sin. That's why he died for those sins, suffered to free
you from the futile burden of trying to resist what you are. It
would be a waste of that sacrifice for you to stop sinning now,
even if you could, which you cannot, and he knew that too. It
would be as if, after hundreds of thousands of soldiers fought
and died for the freedom of African Americans during the
Civil War, they refused to leave the plantations and chose
rather to remain living in servitude. I am telling you now that
you have been enslaved and you are choosing to remain

enslaved by your own fear and ignorance and the lies of those who would use religion to subjugate you! You have been duped and deceived into wasting this precious gift, into believing that sin, which is the natural state of man, is an affront to the Lord who created you to sin. Now, does that make any sense at all?"

"No!"

"I tell you now that to go against your God given nature is to go against God himself! You honor and celebrate our Lord Jesus Christ in your sin! Go forth and be sinful!"

A man dressed in blue jeans, a "Duck Dynasty" t-shirt, with a long oily ponytail sticking out from beneath a baseball cap emblazoned with the Confederate flag, grabbed his emaciated, bruised, and scabbed wife, who looked like she'd been using meth as recently as this morning, and stood up, shouting angrily as he rose.

"You ain't no man of God! You're twisting Jesus's words! This is sacrilegious!"

The guy with the ponytail had barely gotten out the words before a large burly man with a shoulder-length mullet stood up and threw a right hook that connected with his jaw, staggering Ponytail and almost dropping him.

"Dude, what the fuck?" The guy with the ponytail held his jaw, staring at the man who'd struck him in shocked disbelief. He raised his fists to fight back, but the big guy with the mullet hit him again, driving an uppercut into Ponytail's solar plexus that expelled all the air from his lungs. Doubled over, gasping for air, eyes glistening with tears and wide in shock, Ponytail raised his one hand out in front of him in a feeble attempt to ward off further attack while holding his bruised stomach with the other. He heard his wife scream and looked over to see that two overweight-middle-aged women had her by the hair and were punching her repeatedly in the face, pulverizing her features.

"Stop! Stop! Hellllllp! Toby, help me!" His wife screamed, but Toby was in his own world of hurt. A young blonde in a miniskirt with huge, fake tits squeezed into an undersized pink tank top swung a hardback leather-bound hymnal at his head, opening a gash in Toby's forehead. More of the congregation joined in, striking the man with anything they could find. Toby and his meth-head wife wilted beneath a deluge of punches and kicks. Three young toughs, barely out of their teens rushed the couple, two of them baring knives, pushing their way through the crowd of attacking parishioners.

"Oh, God! No! No! Stop! Aaaaah! AAAAAaaaaaah!"

Soon blood and entrails stained the church floor as the couple was disemboweled, their steaming purple intestines, like links of blood sausage, dragged out between the rows of folding chairs.

James remained silent as his flock tore the couple apart.

Several of his regulars took this moment as a cue to begin an orgy, shedding their clothes and furiously fucking in the expanding pool of blood. They bathed their naked bodies in the red river of life pouring forth from their victims, licked it from breasts, cocks, and cunts, used the blood as lube as they filled each other's dripping orifices, adding their own sexual fluids to the tide, swallowing mouthfuls of semen and blood as the culmination of their lusts synchronized with the cessation of life. Ponytail's body still danced in its death throes, stiff limbs rattling spastically against the wood floor as he expired.

James took note of the horrified expressions on the faces of many of the new parishioners. Those were the ones who needed to be converted. Those were the ones who needed most to hear his gospel, to shed the fetters of guilt and morality so they might live salaciously, enjoying all of life's pleasures, awakened to all emotion and sensation. And if they did not convert, if they could not be saved, so brainwashed that they still saw their enslavement as salvation, then they would have to be sacrificed before they could destroy his flock.

"Are there any others who would deny the word of God? Speak now or join in the celebration! Come! Lie down with your brothers and sisters and bathe in the blood of the lamb!

For Christ lives in all of us. This couple's sacrifice shall serve as your communion. Come and receive the sacrament! Be baptized and born anew without fear of sin!"

Each church member was led to the pool of blood in a line and made to strip and be baptized in red. Some came willingly, eagerly shedding their clothes and throwing themselves down amongst the cavorting celebrants to join in the orgy of blood, others wept and offered token resistance, afraid to join in the sin of murder but more terrified of the consequences should they not.

"Be not afraid, my children. Your freedom awaits! By joining us in the ultimate sin, you shall unburden yourselves of your guilt and fear. What is lust or adultery compared to the taking of a life? What is greed or covetousness? Obey your primal instincts, for they are the true commandments of the Lord written into your very genetic code by his divine hand! Look upon the lovely breasts of your neighbor, her supple thighs and sweet pussy. Look upon his firm pecs and biceps, his engorged cock. Feel the lust within you and know that it is good. Allow your desire for the flesh to take you where it will! Be not afraid, for you are children of the Lord made in his divine image. There is no sin but the denial of your natural desires!"

`And one by one, they succumbed to his word, joining the blood orgy until only one remained, terrified and weeping.

***

Holly thought she was losing her mind.

"This can't be happening! What the fuck is going on?"

She hugged herself, weeping and shivering as she watched the death and dismemberment of her friends, Toby and Jessie. She didn't know what she'd expected when she walked through the doors of Our Father Of Perpetual Indulgence, but cowering in a corner listening to her friends scream in pain and agony as they were beaten and stabbed to death was not even in the realm of possibility.

Toby's death was no great loss. If anything, it was a blessing. Toby was an abusive asshole, both verbally and physically, but Jessie had been her best friend since middle school. Holly had been trying to get Jessie to leave that jerk for years, but low self-esteem and a methamphetamine addiction had kept her in place, refusing to leave and taking him back again and again even when he'd broken her jaw and cracked her orbital eye socket, leaving Jessie with one lazy-eye and three missing teeth. Love has reason that reason never knew.

The police were at their house every other weekend, but Toby refused counseling. It was only after Jessie finally pressed charges and Toby spent a weekend in jail and was ordered to attend anger-management classes that he'd agreed to at least go to church. Holly and Jessie had both been hopeful that finding Jesus might change his heart. The same heart now being torn from his chest by a muscular black woman while an equally muscular bald white man fucked her aggressively in her magnificently large round ass. Holly should have known a sexist pig like Toby would choose a sex church to find salvation. He'd probably been hoping he could get Jessie and her into some kind of menage' a trois. He was always trying to stick his little oily cock in her whenever Jessie wasn't around. Once, Holly had let Toby fuck her when he'd promised her an eightball. She had no idea how he always managed to come by such good drugs. Toby could hardly keep a job, but he never seemed to lack money for crack or speed. Holly was certain that was the primary reason Jessie didn't leave him the very first time Toby slapped her around. Meth is a helluva drug.

Once she'd realized what type of place it was, Holly had been about to leave, but something in the Reverend Doctor James Watson's sermon resonated with her, filled her with hope. She had tried to brush off his pretty words, dismiss them as the manipulative fantasies of an expert conman, but it all began to make a bizarre kind of sense to her, and she'd found herself being seduced by his message. Then everything turned into a nightmare.

Holly cringed in the corner, eyes squeezed shut, bony fists pressed against her ears as Jessie's screams wound down to a gurgling death rattle and Toby's corpse finished its convulsions and lay still, no longer the abusive asshole husband of her best friend in the world. Just a bleeding sack of meat and bones.

"Help me, Jesus. Oh, Lord! Sweet Jesus, please help me," Holly mumbled. She didn't know what else to do but pray. She was trapped with a cult of murdering lunatics, too far from the exit to make a run for it without being stopped by one of the Reverend Doctor's followers before she could reach the door, and there was no way she could fight them off. She'd had her last hit of meth more than 48 hours ago, which was like a lifetime for her. She was already feeling sick with withdrawals. Holly was trying to kick cold turkey and was paying in pain for the years of abuse she'd heaped on her body. Chills, nausea, dizziness, body aches, and stomach cramps had plagued her for the last twenty-four hours. Even had she been high, her chances of fighting off the Reverend Doctor's crazed followers would not have been much better. She was fucked, and she knew it. Already she was trying to imagine what it would feel like to be pummeled unconscious then repeatedly stabbed, dismembered, and disemboweled like Toby and Jessie. She began to sob uncontrollably.

"Oh, Jesus. I don't want to die! Help me, God. I'll do anything you ask. You have to help me. Don't let them kill me. Pleeeaaase!"

Her mascara ran down her face like black tears. She rocked back and forth in her little corner, still holding herself, paralyzed with fear.

Holly opened her eyes just as Reverend Doctor James Watson left the pulpit and walked toward her, removing his shirt and pants, a beatific smile spread across his rugged, handsome face. He looked a lot like a punk rock/ biker dude she'd dated in high school. He had been the quintessential "bad boy" and had introduced her to drugs and sex, encouraging her liberal experimentation with both. She imagined he'd look a lot like the Reverend Doctor Watson had he not been immolated when his Harley slid beneath a fuel truck and exploded.

The Reverend Doctor paused and removed his underwear, revealing a thick venous erection bobbing in the air, pointing right at her face like a divining rod. Seeing his huge cock gave Holly an idea, a way to save herself. Perhaps Jesus had answered her prayers after all? This wouldn't be the first time Holly had sucked a cock to get herself out of a bad situation. She'd taken more than one cock down her throat for a hit of meth or crack. If getting face fucked by the good Reverend Doctor Watson would save her life, she'd gladly suck, swallow, and smile. Hell, she'd even gargle with his cum if that's what he wanted.

It's your world, Doc. Just let me live, Holly thought as she crawled toward Reverend Doctor Watson on her hands and knees, affecting the most seductive dick-sucker pucker she could manage.

Holly cleared all thoughts of the carnage she'd witnessed from her mind, focusing on the task at hand, her own survival. Suck a cock and live. It was pretty simple mathematics in her mind. The economics of sex was something she could understand. She wiped the tears from her eyes and beckoned the Reverend Doctor forward with her index finger, then opened her mouth and touched that same finger to her outstretched tongue before sucking on the tip. The reverend was now standing directly above her with his cock throbbing inches from the tip of her nose. She reached up and caressed it.

"Do you not believe? Do you not accept the word of God?" he asked.

Holly shivered but managed to keep a smile on her face as she stroked the reverend's engorged cock, then lightly licked the head.

"I do, Reverend. I accept the word of God. I love God. Let me show you how much."

Slowly, as if the movements caused him discomfort, the Reverend Doctor shook his head. He sighed and a weary half-smile slid upon his narrow face.

"No. You don't accept the word of Christ our Lord. You don't accept me."

Holly slid the head of the Reverend Doctor's cock between her lips, flicking the underside of it with her tongue, licking away a glistening pearl of pre-cum, before swirling her tongue around it. The Reverend Doctor moaned and threw back his head. She continued stroking his cock as she knelt down to lick and suck his balls, taking the wrinkled sack of flesh in her mouth and rolling the testicles around with her tongue one by one. The Reverend Doctor's cock grew even harder, thicker, his moans deepened to a husky growl.

"Oh, how I wish I could believe you, my child."

She could feel he was only minutes away from orgasm when Holly took the Reverend Doctor's cock between her lips once again and inched his turgid flesh to the back of her mouth, past her tonsils, until she could feel his engorged erection pulsating in her throat. Then she grabbed the cult leader by his scrawny buttocks and encouraged him to fuck her mouth. He began with a few tentative thrusts to test her gag reflex. Holly responded like a pro, breathing through her nose when his length clogged her esophagus, licking his cock and stroking it as he slid it back out so the head of his cock was encircled by her lips before sliding it back down her throat with increasing urgency. Tears wept from Holly's eyes as the Reverend Doctor raped her throat. More mascara ran down her face, drawing long black lines, turning her cheeks into a spiderweb of dark shadows. The Reverend Doctor grabbed the back of her head in both hands, ramming his cock violently to the back of her throat, brutally fucking her mouth. His body tensed, and he threw back his head, staring heaven-ward as he began to jerk and spasm.

"Oh, God! Oh, my sweet Christ our Lord. I'm cumming! I'm cumming, Father!" He cried out as his seed filled Holly's mouth and she dutifully gulped it down, licking spilled semen from her lips, scooping it from her chin with her hand and sucking her fingers clean. The Reverend Doctor reached down and, with a hand beneath each of her arms, raised her to her feet. He hugged her, brushed her hair from her face, then kissed her forehead.

"Oh, my child you are a wonder!" He laughed, smiling joyously.

Holly forced herself to smile, stifling her sobs. She wiped the back of her hand across her eyes, smearing dark makeup from eye to temples and blackening the back of her hand. She touched her bruised lips gently. Her mouth felt like she'd been smacked.

"I told you I'm faithful. I love Christ. I can love you too, any way you like," Holly said, congratulating herself on a job well done. She had saved her life with the most basic of skills, a simple blowjob. Empires had crumbled, wars had been won, marriages ended, and relationships born on the power of that one simple act. Her father may have been an asshole, but he'd saved her life today by teaching her that. May he rot in prison forever, she thought.

The Reverend Doctor's smile bristled with malevolence as he placed his palms on both sides of Holly's face and forced eye contact, peering deep into her bloodshot baby blues.

"I believe you are the one. You and I are going to do something wonderful together. Come with me," the Reverend Doctor said. He gestured to two blood-drenched acolytes who'd been watching their entire exchange intently, presumably prepared to rush to his defense and end her life had she been stupid enough to try something like biting off the Reverend Doctor's cock and spitting it in his face. She had certainly been tempted to do just that but saw no way in which that ended well for her. One of the men was a stocky, hyper-muscular black guy with biceps as large as Holly's head.

The other was a tall, lean, but well-built blond who towered a full head above his partner and at least a foot above Holly.

The Reverend Doctor's other lunatic followers were still fucking, sucking, stroking, and licking on the church floor. They were all covered in tacky coagulating blood, but none of them seemed to mind. Holly stared at them longingly, wondering if she might not have been better off joining in with their orgy as she was led to the back of the church and into another room. She cast one last glance at her two dead friends. Jesse had been completely decapitated, one of the congregants was fucking her disembodied head while two other men raped her corpse, one was fucking her headless throat, grunting like a beast as he came down her vandalized neck-hole. Toby, who'd always been a racist, sexist, homophobic piece of shit, was suffering the most fitting indignity she could imagine as his corpse was brutally sodomized by the mullet-wearing brute who'd been the first to strike him. A morbidly-obese African-American woman with huge pendulous breasts the size of watermelons and an ass like a beach-ball sat upon Toby's lifeless face, grinding her blood-soaked pussy against his mouth. Holly could not tell if it was Toby's blood that coated the woman's dripping snatch or if the blood was coming out of her. Holly turned away, and the door was shut and locked behind her.

She looked around the room she'd entered. There were a few candles glowing in the windowless room, but it was otherwise dark. Slowly, her eyes adjusted to the gloom, and Holly began to scream.

"No! No! Noooo! Nooooo!"

The room was filled with torture devices. Holly had been to a BDSM dungeon once in her life, and she recognized many of the implements hanging from the walls, whips, floggers, paddles, straps, canes, all things she recalled vividly from that painful night with the wrong trick. There was a chair with leather restraints at the arms and legs, a standing cross also affixed with chains and metal shackles. A dentist chair filled one corner of the room with a tray full of sharp implements beside it. There was a stockade, a huge spider web of chains stretched between a big wooden octagon frame large enough to suspend a human being from, a leather bondage table, and many other terrible pieces of furniture.

Holly struggled to escape, tugging on the doorknob. The Reverend Doctor's two blood-soaked followers dragged her away from the door and toward a leather-topped table that had handcuffs at the top two corners and ankle cuffs at the bottom corners. The big black guy who was built like a linebacker took hold of both of her wrists, crushing them together in one of his huge hands. One at a time, he locked them into the handcuffs. Holly thrashed and kicked at the tall blond guy, catching him with a kick to the chest that staggered him back and seemed to knock the wind out of him. He recovered and seized one of her ankles, struggling to lock it into the cuffs as Holly continued to fight and struggle. This time she connected with a kick to the tall man's jaw that knocked him to the floor, where he laid unconscious for several seconds before raising to a sitting position. Holly felt a momentary thrill of victory and hope before the big linebacker grabbed her by both ankles and, ignoring her kicks and struggles, easily wrestled her into the restraints. Once she was completely helpless, he stepped away, then turned to help his tall friend up from the floor.

"Heeeelp! Heeeelp!" Holly cried out.

"Shhhhh!" The Reverend Doctor said as he approached the table and ran a hand up her inner thigh. "You are about to experience something few people on earth ever have. Do you know what I did before I started this church? I was a psychologist. My specialty was addictions and so-called deviant sexual issues, but after several years counseling drug-addicts, I developed my own opioid addiction. Just like you. I sank as low as a human being possibly can. I was living in the gutter, stealing, even prostituting myself to support my habit. Sound familiar? I went from prescription pain-killers to heroin. It took finding God for me to finally kick my dependency. And, like so many of the newly saved, I began reading the bible fanatically. I was addicted to God. He became my new drug. It was during my sixth or seventh cover to cover read of The New Testament that I had my revelation, that the true meaning of The Resurrection was revealed to me. I felt compelled to spread the good word. That's why I built this church."

Holly's brow knitted in confusion. Eyes wide, she shook her head

"What? What the fuck does that have to do with me? Why am I chained up?"

Reverend Doctor James Watson nodded.

"I'm sure this must all be confusing for you. Let me try to explain. See, before my fall from grace, I was a respected psychologist. In addition to treating patients for their various addictions, I also did a lot of research studies, conducted a lot of experiments. I had a theory that I never got to test. Have you ever heard of the bliss point?"

Holly slowly shook her head.

"In the food industry, the bliss point is the most pleasurable, the most addictive amount of sugar you can add to food before it starts to become less enjoyable, the point at which the most pleasure is derived. Too little, and it is good, but not as good as it could be. Too much, and you reach a point of diminishing returns where the experience actually begins to lose pleasure by degrees. It just becomes too sweet. See, I was convinced that all physical sensation had a bliss point, not just taste but cutaneous and subcutaneous sensations as well–even sexual pleasure. There has to be a point beyond which pleasure becomes pain. And, conversely, a point at which pain becomes pleasure, where the endorphin levels reach a point that they overcome the pain. Did you know they have conducted experiments with monkeys where they hooked the pleasure centers of their brains up to electrodes and gave them a button to push that would send a current through their brains that would simulate an orgasm? Those monkeys kept pushing that button until it fried their brains and killed them. I believe those monkeys wanted to die. Even back then, when I was just a psychologist, before I had ever found God, I was convinced that this bliss point is what man calls heaven, nirvana, rapture ... and hell. I believe those monkeys reached a point where they could see heaven, and I believe you and I will reach that point together today."

Holly began to struggle again, terrified of what his words meant for her.

"What are you going to do to me? Please, please just let me go! Don't hurt me! Please!"

"That's just it. I don't want to hurt you. I don't want to only hurt you. I want to give you true bliss. Oh, and don't think I'm arrogant enough to think I can do this all on my own. I have no illusions of my own sexual prowess. I have many wonderful devices here to help."

***

Holly screamed and moaned, ' thrashing against her restraints as one orgasm after another wracked her body with violent convulsions that were almost agonizing. The Reverend Doctor's two brutes had fixed a spreader bar between her ankle cuffs and strapped her thighs down to the table with two big leather restraints, making it impossible for her to close her legs or move them much at all. Another thick strap, like an old-fashioned weightlifter's belt, went around her waist, holding her firmly against the table, limiting her movement from the waist down. She cried and pleaded the entire time, promising them all the best blowjobs of their lives if they would just let her go, an eternity of blowjobs.

"You can fuck me in the ass if you want! I'll take all three of you at once, double- penetration, ass-to-mouth, any nasty filthy fantasy you can imagine. We can turn it into a bukakke session. You can all cum on my face. I'll suck all of you dry, then get you hard again so we can do it all over again. I promise. Just let me go!"

She could tell that the tall guy and the linebacker were considering her proposal from the lengthening and thickening of their enormous cocks, but it wasn't them she needed to convince. They were just followers, and their leader had already cum once. His cock hung limply between his scrawny pale thighs. Holly wept, realizing she'd played her only bargaining chip too soon.

"You are good, my child. So good. I can't remember the last time a woman worshiped my cock like that, but I can get that from any and every woman in my congregation if that's all I wanted. We have a higher purpose here. I want you to enter heaven, to see the face of God. That's the only way to make you a true believer."

A device Holly recognized as a Hitachi Magic Wand (the Cadillac of vibrators) was strapped into a leather harness. There was something different about it, though. She had one of the powerful devices in her bedroom at home, and it didn't look quite like this thing.

"This is an electro vibe wand. It vibrates just as power-fully as the famous Magic Wand, but it also delivers powerful electric shocks. It has five different intensity levels. I believe we are going to hit all five. But first ..."

The big muscular black guy, the linebacker, handed the Reverend Doctor a small black box with lots of wires hanging from it.

"This is a tens unit. They use it during physical therapy. It sends electric currents through your muscles to make them contract."

"What are you going to do with it?" Holly asked, watching him affix little metal alligator clamps to the ends of each wire. She cried out when he attached the clamps to her labia and nipples. He affixed little sticky pads to four more leads and slid two of them up inside her, attaching them to the walls of her vagina, then fixing the last two to her anus.

The Reverend Doctor held up a pear-shaped metal device

that also had wires attached to it. Holly recognized it as a buttplug–a vibrating buttplug.

"And finally, a simple metal vibrator ... attached to a Violet Wand electrostimulator."

He slathered the vibrator, the buttplug, her asshole, and her entire vagina with a conductive gel that also served as a lubricant, then slid both the metal vibrator and the plug up inside her. The vibrations immediately began to do their job, sending delicious sensations throughout her sex. Jacked up on fear and adrenaline, her body began to betray her, rapidly approaching orgasm. She had been terrified at first that they were going to torture and kill her, finding out that they only wanted her to cum her brains out was definitely an improvement. She decided to just let it happen, not to fight it. Hell, she thought, she might even enjoy it. Then the Reverend Doctor turned on the tens unit, and her vagina began to rhythmically contract. Her nipples were buzzing like she was hooked up to a car battery, which was essentially exactly what she was wired to. Unable to fight it, the first violent orgasm tore through her, surprising her and stealing her breath away. Had she not been strapped down, she felt like she would have flown off the table. Holly could not remember when she'd had such a powerful climax, if ever. She was panting heavily like she'd just run a mile in an all-out sprint, but the Reverend Doctor was not done. She had forgotten about the Hitachi. He strapped the harness around her hips and thighs, holding the large vibrator firmly against her clitoris. Then he turned it on.

Holly's dilated rectum and vaginal walls were contracting around the vibrator and the buttplug buzzing inside her as the tens unit did its job, the Hitachi buzzed against her clitoris, her labia and nipples vibrated with electricity. Holly screamed as another orgasm ripped through her and she continued to cum, one bone-jarring climax after another, tumbling down over each other like an avalanche of pleasure, buffeting her body relentlessly. Whenever she thought she could not experience any more pleasure, the Reverend Doctor would turn up the intensity on the tens unit or the Hitachi, driving her further and further into a cocoon of overwhelming ecstasy. Holly was delirious. She had no idea how long she'd been in the room or how many orgasms she'd endured. A river of vaginal fluid flowed between her legs, saturating the leather bondage table.

"Oh, my God! Oh, fuck! Oh, Jesus Christ! I can't take it anymore! Stop! Please stop! I feel like I'm dying!" Her eyes rolled up in her head, saliva drooled from the corners of her mouth, and tears flowed freely as she continued to cum.

"Do you see him? Do you see the face of God?" the Reverend Doctor asked, bristling with excitement.

Holly shook her head from side to side, then thought better of it and began to nod enthusiastically.

"Yes! Yes, I see him! I do! He's beautiful!"

The Reverend Doctor dropped his head, closed his eyes and let out a long sigh.

"No. You don't see him. You're lying. Don't lie to me. This will all go so much better if you are truthful."

Holly sobbed loudly, uncontrollably.

"Just let me go! Let me go! You have to stop! I can't take it!"

She could barely see the maniacal cult leader through the haze of salacious sensations. His voice sounded like it was a mile away. Holly was dimly aware that the two brutes were masturbating on either side of her. They splattered her face and breasts with cum that dripped down her forehead into her eyes. She tried to blink the sticky mess away. When she could see again, she saw that they were still masturbating, preparing to ejaculate on her again.

"Then you have to tell me the truth. I want to know when you pass through the gates of heaven. I want to know when you see the Lord's face."

"I'm not lying! I see him! I do!" Holly said breathlessly, another orgasm colliding against her like a wall, knocking her head back and causing her entire body to spasm and convulse.

"No. I'm afraid you aren't quite there yet. Let's turn it up a bit more shall we?"

"Please! Please don't! I can't take anymore! I'll die! You're killing me!"

Electric shocks ripped through her loins as the metal vibrator inside her began to crackle with electricity and the Hitachi strapped against her clitoris released its own electric charge, as did the metal buttplug vibrating deep in her anus. The pain was intense, but combined with the powerful vibrations, the painful jolts brought her to more thunderous orgasms that felt like they would break her in half. Her mind swam in a sea of agony and ecstasy, going under, slowly drowning in sensations beyond anything she could have imagined.

A joyous smile burst upon her face and Holly whispered, "More."

The Reverend Doctor leaned in closer.

"What did you say, child?"

"Don't stop. Please, don't stop. I want more. I want more! More!"

The Reverend smiled and nodded. "Ahhh, the Bliss Point."

He turned up the intensity on the electro wand between her legs all the way to five, then turned up the tens unit and the Violet Wand until Holly's entire body crackled and hummed with electricity and the smell of burning flesh filled the air along with the pheromone rich musk of sex. When the Reverend Doctor removed a scalpel and a cauterizing pen from a medical bag and began cutting and burning her, Holly could no longer distinguish the pain from the pleasure. It had all merged into one kaleidoscope of lubricious sensation. She was drunk, intoxicated with endorphins, only dimly aware that she was still cumming, that she was still in the dark room strapped to the table, who she was or had ever been, as the

Reverend Doctor cut a circle around Holly's left breast then grabbed the edges of her skin with a hemostats and slowly removed the skin with a wet, sticky ripping sound, peeling it like a grape and revealing the bubbly yellow fat and pink muscle tissue beneath. The two brutes were still furiously masturbating as they crowded in to watch their beloved religious leader skin Holly's breast.

"I see Him!" Holly shouted. "I see the face of God!" she repeated gleefully, smiling in profound joy, divine rapture, as semen rained down upon her ecstatic face.

Chapter Thirteen

HORSE

"When the lamb opened the second seal, I heard the second beast say, "Come!" Then another, a fiery red horse of bloodshed, came out; and its rider was empowered to take peace from the earth, so that men would slaughter one another, and a great sword of war and violent death was given to him."

— REVELATION 6:3-4

"Yo, why do they call it horse when it ain't even white? Is this shit even real heroin? Why the fuck is it red?" the kid asked.

Dicky was just shy of his twenty-third birthday, so "kid" was an entirely subjective description. But the kid still lived in the same house he grew up in, same bedroom he'd had since he was a toddler. The walls were covered in hip-hop posters, video game posters, horror and sci-fi movie posters, and centerfolds. Action figures, well-worn comic books, old sports memorabilia, and used equipment cluttered the shelves, and soiled clothes littered the floors. According to his birth certificate, he may have been twenty-two years old, but Dicky's emotional and mental maturity had been arrested the day he'd smoked his first joint at thirteen. That joint had been followed quickly by crack, heroin, and meth. Now, he seemed to bounce indecisively between the three.

I'm not suggesting that weed was some sort of gateway drug and Dicky would have been some regular dude if he'd never smoked a joint. That's a bunch of conservative propaganda bullshit. Nope. Dicky was never going to turn out right. There was something wrong with him from the start. I mean, what kid starts drinking hard liquor at age nine, trying to fuck his own eight-year-old sister at age twelve, and robbing old ladies and sucking dick for crack before his first day of high school? Dicky was fucked from the day he slid out his mom's snatch. He wasn't ever going to be right, with or without the drugs.

"Yo, chill, Dicky. This ain't heroin. I never said I had heroin. I said I had horse. This is some new shit. The government been giving this shit to soldiers to make them like super soldiers or some shit. It's supposed to make you feel like motherfucking superman, yo!"

That's not really how I talk, but you have to know how to code-switch to be a successful drug dealer. I can't walk into the hood flashing my master's degree in business management. They'd think I was a narc. Talking like a Columbia University graduate wouldn't do shit but just get my ass shot. So, I save the queen's English for when I head back to my family in the suburbs at the end of the day.

"How'd you get this shit, and why ain't I ever heard of it?" Dicky asked.

"You ain't never heard of it because you too high all the time to watch the news. All you do is watch cartoons and porn all day. But this shit is everywhere, yo. It's the hottest shit on the streets right now."

I wasn't lying. One day, everyone was fiending for crack, meth, and heroin. The next day, the streets were ringing with people fiending for "that red shit." I don't know how it got the name horse, but it stuck. There were rumors that the CIA was pumping this shit into the ghettos. That it was some sort of genocidal plot to wipe out poor people and minorities. I don't know about all that. All I know is ever since I got laid off from the corporation I had given ten years of my life to, horse is the only thing keeping the lights on and food on the table.

"Man, I just want some heroin. I don't trust that red shit. How I know it won't make me sick?"

"How'd you know heroin wouldn't the first time you tried it? Or crack? Or even weed? You didn't. You wanted to get high, so you just gave that shit a try."

"Why you pushin' this shit so hard, yo? Just give me some regular ass heroin! You said you had some, and then you come at me with this shit!"

"Ain't nobody sellin' heroin no more. No more crack. No more meth. Don't nobody want that shit no more. Everybody be wantin' horse now. You can't get that old shit nowhere."

I wasn't lying about that either. It was like horse had done what the entire federal government and local law enforcement had been unable to do for the past 60 years, get heroin and cocaine off the streets. Hell, the local news was practically running commercials for the stuff. I first heard about it on a special news report.

"There's a new drug sweeping through the inner city. The drug is called 'horse' and it is supposed to be stronger and more addictive than meth, with a high that last ten times longer. Oddly enough, there have been no reported cases of anyone overdosing on the drug. There does not appear to be a dosage that would be considered lethal as far as doctors can tell; however, extreme paranoia and aggression caused by the drug has led to a dramatic increase in violence all over the city ..."

The very next day after that report aired on the six-o'clock news, every dope-fiend on the street was clamoring for that shit. And, I swear with god as my witness, that I hadn't seen a drop of the shit on the street before that news report aired. Not a whisper or a rumor of it. It was like they created the demand first and then dropped the product.

It hadn't been hard for me to find a connection for it. I asked one crackhead, who pointed me to another, who pointed me to a dealer, who pointed me to his connection. And I'm going to tell you right now, it ain't ever that easy. You don't just walk up to a dealer on the street and say you want to buy a kilo of anything and they just introduce you to their connection without vetting you and sweating you. The whole thing was just fucking weird. But the money? That shit was good. I made more in a week selling horse than I used to make in a month selling heroin. But even I could see the results. Shit was getting scary in the city, and now this shit had spread to the suburbs.

I heard a congressman's daughter shot a Muslim baker after shouting anti-Islamic insults at him. She'd known the guy for years, been going to his bakery every morning for coffee and croissants. Then one day she just snapped. Her father said it was the drugs. I laughed that shit off at first, but then I started to notice it too. People were tripping on this shit.

"Okay ... well ... I ain't payin' for shit unless I get a taste first."

"You know I don't work that way. Look, you don't want none? Don't buy none. But, I'm tellin' you, you ain't gonna find nothing else out here, and at least you know with me, it ain't gonna be cut with nothing crazy."

"All right. All right! Fuck it! Give me an ounce."

He handed me twenty dollars in crumpled ones. I handed him a gram of horse.

"So, what do you do? You just shoot this shit up like heroin? Sniff it? Eat it?"

"All of the above. It works the same either way. Probably hit you quicker if you shot it up, but if you snort it, you ain't got to worry about catching the HIV from a dirty needle, you feel me?"

"Yeah, yeah, true dat."

Dicky opened the little ball of aluminum foil I'd sold him, looked around to make sure no one was watching, as if anyone would care, then pushed his right nostril closed with his finger and took a deep snort of the red dust with his left nostril. As if I could already anticipate what was about to happen, I put my hand in my jacket pocket and gripped my Berretta. I clicked off the safety and put my finger on the trigger. That's when Dicky's eyes turned red.

"Whoa! This shit is intense. I feel like going on a faggot killing spree right now, killing every cocksucker in the world!"

"What the fuck did you just say, motherfucker?" I asked.

"You heard me, cocksucker. I'm going to bash your fucking brains in then fuck you in the ass, you gay motherfucker!"

I don't know how he knew. I had always been really good at "playing straight." I even thought I had the hardcore, cis-het, gangsta image pretty well established. I guess I was wrong.

"You better watch who you talkin' to like that, 'cause I ain't the one."

"Oh, don't play with me, motherfucker. Everybody knows you got a boyfriend up there in the suburbs where you stay at. You ain't foolin' nobody! I'm going to ass-rape your corpse!"

"And, you don't see anything wrong with threatening to anally rape me for being gay?" I said, slowly pulling the gun from my pocket. This batch of horse was a lot stronger than the last. I hadn't seen anyone get so agro after just one hit before. I knew something about the drug seemed to bring out people's prejudices and make them act violently. But, it usually took a few days of constant use to really get them riled up. I guess whoever made this shit thought that was too long and decided to rev it up.

Dicky snatched the metal lid off a nearby trashcan and swung it at my head. I shot him in the chest a moment before his blow landed. We both fell. Everything went black for a second, and when it cleared again, I was lying on my back in the alley, bleeding from my forehead and from the back of my head where it had struck the concrete. Dicky was laying across from me, trembling and shaking in his death throes, a gurgling and whistling sound coming from his mouth as blood bubbled up out of it. Well, at the very least, that ought to give me a little street-cred, I thought.

I struggled to my feet. My head ached, and I was still dizzy. Obviously a concussion. A bad one. Luckily, my car was only half a block away. I had paid one of the neighborhood junkies to watch it for me like I always do. One dollar now, and a dollar when I come back and my car hasn't been stolen or vandalized. I wasn't positive I would even be able to drive in my present condition, but I knew I didn't want to be caught down here with a body, the murder weapon, and a fanny pack full of horse. I wondered if maybe it was the fanny pack that had given me away, but then I dismissed that. Most straight people thought all gay men had excellent fashion sense. A gay nerd selling drugs in the hood, pretending to be a gangster was absurd enough that no one should have been able to imagine it, let alone believe it. That's what I'd told Michael, my husband, when I first let him in on my plan for our financial salvation.

"You're going to get yourself killed," Michael said.

"Well, you want me to sell drugs to our friends? How would that look? You want our neighbors knowing you're married to a drug dealer?"

"Don't be a fucking drug dealer! There are other options."

"Like what? I have been sending out ten resumes a day for over three months. No one is calling. No one is hiring. We miss another mortgage payment and we lose this house. You want us to be the cute, gay, homeless couple? You ready for life on the streets? Because I'm not."

After a few more such discussions, Michael relented. Once we got caught up on our mortgage, then paid off the house entirely, and bought two brand new SUVs, he really seemed to enjoy being married to a successful drug dealer. But Michael didn't know anything about what this drug does to people. He thought it was just a harmless party drug like Ecstasy. He hadn't seen the pure hatred that comes with the euphoria. The rage that accompanies the rush.

Old Willie, the middle-aged junkie I had paid to watch my BMW, had obviously tried his best to earn that extra dollar. My car had been destroyed, completely vandalized, but so had Willie. His entrails decorated the roof of the car with a garland of gore. His disembodied head had been placed on the dashboard with his own cock and balls crammed into his mouth, eyes gored out, nose smashed, and almost every last tooth knocked out. Various internal organs were strewn around the vehicle in pools of coagulating red ichor as if Old Willie had been a piñata filled with blood and viscera and someone had taken a bat and a hatchet to him in their eagerness to claim the goodies inside. The rest of him sat behind the wheel of the car, his chest torn open like an oyster that had been cracked, shucked, and bled all over. He had been gutted. His chest and abdominal cavities were completely empty. It almost looked like it had been licked clean.

The car hood was open, and the battery, radiator, and most of the engine were gone. What remained had been smashed or torn out and tossed to the ground. Loose wires and hoses dangled everywhere, dripping oil, wiper fluid, engine coolant, and blood. Willie's blood. Written in blood and oil, on the inside of the hood, and repeated on the passenger-side door, were the words "Go Back To Mexico!" Which was odd because I'm not Mexican. I'm not even Spanish.

I knew I was in shock. That, along with the concussion still clouding my thoughts and causing my head to pound in agony, may have explained why I stood there for so long just staring at Old Willie's corpse, trying to make sense of what I was seeing, not fully registering the horror of it, wondering how I could drive a car home with slashed tires, a shattered windshield, a missing engine, and a headless corpse in the driver's seat.

"Men! Fucking men! Rapists! Fascists! Fucking wife-beaters and baby-rapers!"

I looked across the street, tearing my eyes away from the massacre that had taken place inside my BMW. On the opposite sidewalk, a woman was stabbing a man with a kitchen knife as he batted and punched at her in a feeble effort to defend himself. The woman had her hair in rollers, some of which had fallen out, and she wore a robe over a diaphanous gown that did little to cover her massive breasts, which flopped up to her chin then back down to her belly with each rise and fall of the knife. She was bleeding from her nose, and her lip was swollen. I wasn't sure if the damage to her face had inspired her rampage or if they had been wounds inflicted by her victim's fruitless attempt to fend her off. The woman grabbed the man by the hair, then began sawing at his throat as he flopped and convulsed like a dying fish. A horrible gargling sound came from his throat while he was slowly decapitated.

"Oh, shit. What the fuck is going on?"

But I knew. It was the horse. That new red shit. It was driving people insane. And, moreover, I was absolutely certain now that that's exactly what it had been created to do. The conspiracy theorists were correct. The CIA or some other government operatives had deliberately dumped that shit in the ghetto to make all the poor folks kill each other.

"I've got to get out of here," I muttered to no one. There was no one there to help me, no one to rescue me. Michael was a good thirty miles away. That was a forty-five-minute drive in traffic. I could call him, but he'd never make it in time to save me, and I'd be putting his life in danger too. Of course,

I could call the cops, but I had just murdered someone in a drug deal. Even if I ditched the gun and the drugs, something I was hesitant to do with all the chaos roaring around me, there would still be gunpowder residue all over me, and I would have to explain what the fuck I was doing down here in the first place. My best bet was to make my way to the nearest bus stop and pray it came quick. Once I was somewhere less dangerous, I could call an Uber or something to get home. Then, I'd have to tell Michael what happened to the car. I'd have to tell him everything. He wouldn't be happy. He'd want me to stop. But, if I stopped selling horse, the cash flow would also end. We'd be right back where we started. None of that mattered now, though. I was thinking too much, wasting time. I had already stood in one place too long. The woman who'd just sawed that dude's head off was walking toward me now.

"Rapist!" she screamed, pointing her blood-spattered carving knife directly at me.

"Rapist? Me? Honey, I'm gay. And, unless you've got a cock and balls under there, you ain't got nothing that interests me, girl," I said, queening it up and feeling a little ill for doing so. Just like my fake gangster voice, my "gay" voice was an amalgamation of stereotypes. I was doing the LGBTQ version of a minstrel show. But if it kept this crazy bitch from trying to saw my head off, and me from having to make yet another body, I could finger-pop and neck roll with the best of them.

The woman paused, squinting her eyes and studying me, trying to process what I'd just told her. I put one hand on my hip, cocked that hip to the side, then lifted my other hand, wrist limp and dangling almost lifelessly, before I snapped my fingers four times making a "Z" in the air like I was a gay Zorro. I felt as ridiculous as it sounds. My face reddened with shame, but it seemed to work. The woman lowered the blade.

"Gay? Like queer?"

Finally, it was sinking in.

"As queer as a three-dollar bill, girl," I said, adding another snap in the air for emphasis.

"Did a man do that? Did he hurt you?" she asked, pointing to the gash on my forehead. I reached up and touched the wound. It was still bleeding profusely.

I nodded.

"Yes. Yes, a man did this."

"They're fucking animals. They're all fucking animals," she said.

I nodded again. "Yes. Yes, they fucking are."

She cocked her head like a dog listening to a strange sound.

"What are you doing here? You don't belong down here. You're going to get yourself killed."

"I'm just trying to get home to my husband."

"Did he do that to you?"

"No. He's a good man."

"There are no fucking good men!" she yelled, raising the knife again.

"I-I mean he's gay ... like me."

She nodded.

"Yeah. Gay dudes are cool. I ain't never been hurt by no fag–I mean–a gay person."

I thought it was odd that a woman who'd just decapitated a man would be worried about offending me by accidentally using a homophobic slur. It was almost as odd as me standing in the middle of the street having a conversation with someone who'd just sawed a dude's head off in front of me.

"Okay, well ... I have to get home. My husband's going to be worried to death."

"It's not safe. But, I'll get you home. I'll protect you. We on the same side, right?"

"Right," I said. Who was I to argue? Besides, it wasn't like I couldn't use the help.

She wrapped a belt around her blood-drenched robe, then took my hand and began leading me away.

"I need to get to a bus stop. They destroyed my car."

"We'll get you another car," she said. And I knew better

than to ask how. I suspected I was going to be party to another felony whether I liked it or not.

"My name's Melody," the woman said, switching the kitchen knife to her left hand so she could offer me her right hand to shake. Her fingers still dripped with blood, but I shook her hand anyway. There was no sense in me being sensitive about it. We were all killers tonight.

"My name's Brandon."

"Pleased to meet you, Brandon. You just follow me. I'll get you out of here. And, I'll kill any motherfucker that tries to stop me!" Melody screamed into the night.

I immediately began having second thoughts.

We hadn't walked more than a few blocks before the sounds of screams and gunfire echoed all around us. Angry shouts and curses, the smack and thud of fists against flesh, bodies falling to the pavement. I watched a gang of teenagers drag a man through the streets, chained to their low rider. We passed an alley where a stocky middle-aged man was beating some dude to death with his bare fists, muttering "baby-raper" and "fucking pedophile" as he pulverized the frail-looking man, who looked well into his late forties or early fifties. We paused for a second to watch as the big guy pulled down the other man's pants, then took a broomstick and rammed it so far up the guy's asshole that blood exploded from his mouth.

"Serve's that piece of shit right," Melody said.

I didn't know if the guy had actually been guilty or not, and neither did she. He looked like a pedophile, white, balding, beady eyes, pencil neck with a bulging Adam's apple, thick glasses, pants too tight, pinstriped polo shirt buttoned all the way up to his throat. If I saw him on the street, I'd have thought he was a baby-raper too. But that didn't mean he was guilty. If he was, then he definitely deserved it, though.

"Fuck you, bitch-ass nigga!"

"Kill that white boy!"

"Goddamn spic!"

"Fuckin' stank ho!"

"Chink!"

"Wetback!"

"Sand nigger!"

"Jew!"

"Greasy dago!"

"Slut!"

"Whore!"

"Fag!"

"Pig!"

"Liberal commie snowflake!"

"Fascist repugnican!"

Every ounce of bigotry, prejudice, intolerance, and hatred in the entire neighborhood was bubbling to the surface. Not everyone in the neighborhood was high on horse, but enough to light the spark. After that, mass hysteria, mob mentality, a primordial, tribal, groupthink had taken over. Nothing galvanizes people like hatred. Small insignificant differences and divisions became insurmountable chasms, reasons to fight, kill, or die. Anyone who didn't look like them, think like them, dress like them, worship like them, or vote like them was now the enemy. Blood was being spilled in every direction I looked.

We reached Germantown Avenue. The Ave was an open-air drug market. Two separate gangs slung rocks, coke, and heroin with impunity. Eastsiders on the east side of the street. Westsiders on the west side. In between, dope fiends, crack-heads, and tweakers wandered back and forth, bargain shopping. But not today.

Today, drug addicts attacked dealers, fighting them for more horse, killing them for it. Two tweakers who weighed less than two hundred pounds combined were tearing open a teenaged dealer with their teeth and nails, one chewed at his face, tearing off his cheeks, nose, and eyelids, while his homeboy eviscerated the man, clawing open his stomach and pulling out his entrails in handfuls. An older man with a huge graying afro was beating a gangbanger with a cane. The gangster's skull had already caved in, but the old man continued whacking him with the cane, reducing the guy's head to a misshapen blob of red pulp and white bone.

The sound of gunshots echoed out, and I looked up to see a group of nearly twenty men carrying shotguns, semi-automatic handguns, and military-style assault rifles, Ak-47s, MAC-10s, Uzis, and AR-15s. They wore sagging jeans with bandannas on their heads and wrapped around their heavily tattooed faces. The men were mowing down people indiscriminately as they strutted, swaggered, and strolled forward. Heads, torsos, and limbs blew apart in sprays of blood and meat. The men continued to advance, killing everything in their path.

Six patrol cars roared into the intersection of Washington Lane and Germantown Avenue. For a brief moment, hope swelled in my chest. I was just about to run over to them when I felt a hand on my shoulder, pulling me back. It was Melody. Her eyes were still blood-red, but there was less madness in her eyes now. Or perhaps that was just what I wanted to see.

"Don't," she said.

"It's the cops! They can help us!" I cried out, nearly hysterical. I didn't care anymore that I was carrying enough schedule 1 narcotics to put me away for twenty years, or that I had a murder weapon in my pocket. I just wanted out.

"Look," was her only response. She pointed to the cops exiting their vehicles in riot gear, carrying shotguns, some carried M-16 assault rifles. They were ready for war.

"They ain't here to help nobody." Melody's voice was calm and steady. Despite the narcotics firing uncut hatred through her synapses, she seemed to be thinking clearer than I was at the moment.

The police officers began opening fire, killing men, women, and children alike, marching toward the group of gangbangers, sandwiching civilians between the two small armies, cutting them to pieces with gunfire.

"They're killing everyone!" I shouted.

"No shit, Sherlock," Melody said, and just then a man stepped out of the alley behind us, carrying a revolver, aiming it at the center of Melody's chest. He had those same blood-red eyes Melody had, the same look Dicky had on his face right before he tried to decapitate me with a trashcan lid.

"Cheating whore!" he yelled. I thought maybe he was her husband or boyfriend, but the confusion on Melody's face made it clear. She had no fucking idea who he was.

"Fool, I don't know you! And who the fuck are you calling a whore?!"

"You, skank bitch!"

If sanity had begun to creep into Melody's eyes earlier, it was now scattered like grains of sand in a tsunami. I tried to swat the gun out of the man's hand, feeling protective of this madwoman who had vowed to protect me. Then she sank her knife deep into the man's chest with much more force than her skinny arms should have been capable of. I heard the man's sternum crack, the knife crunch through muscle and bone before embedding itself deep in his lungs. Melody wrenched it free and then repeated the action, this time aiming for his heart. I watched the life flee from that man's eyes like his soul had been little more than an annoying insect that Melody had casually shooed away. His empty carcass collapsed at our feet, an empty sack of meat. It made a wet smack on the concrete.

"Let's go," Melody said.

"Where? I don't know where to go! The bus stop is right there where those cops are killing everyone!"

"Well, then we definitely can't go there," Melody said.

"Well, no shit we can't go there!"

"Why are you yelling at me, Brandon?" I saw something dark slither across her red pupils. As if there was something in there with her, something sharing space in her body that had peeked out for a minute. She was still clutching that knife, wet with yet another man's blood.

"Nuh – uh – nothing. Nothing. Just tell me where to go. I need your help."

"Well, how the fuck should I know where to go?! Why the fuck are you asking me? First you yell at me, then you want my help? Fuck you, Brandon!" Melody shouted, pointing the knife at me. She was getting crazy. My testicles crept up tight against my body, and a chill of fear raced down my spine. Melody was about to kill me. I knew it. I could feel an itch in the center of my chest, right where I knew she was intending to stick that knife.

"Can I call my husband? Please?" It was the only thing I could think to say. I knew I was going to die. I just wanted to hear his voice one more time before it all went away, before everything I was became nothing. I still had the Beretta. I probably could have shot her. Maybe. But I just didn't think I'd be fast enough. I knew I wouldn't be. If she was going to kill me, then I was going to die. It was as certain to me as the ground under my feet.

"What?"

"I ... I just want to call my husband. Please. Please let me call him?"

Her expression softened. A little of the madness left her eyes.

"Shh-Sure. Sure. Okay. I ain't stopping you."

I began to cry. Tears wept from my eyes, one, two, and then a river. I was sobbing uncontrollably as I fumbled my phone out of my pocket, dropping the Beretta. I called Michael. He answered on the first ring.

"Brandon! Where are you? You have to get home. I'm scared. I need you. Everything's going crazy over here! Everyone's killing each other!"

"What?"

"People are killing each other. The neighbors are going door-to-door killing everybody!"

It wasn't just the ghettoes. It was happening everywhere.

"Just stay inside. Keep the door locked."

"I need you here, Brandon. I need you with me. You're supposed to protect me. You're supposed to take care of me!"

He was right. I was the big, bad drug dealer. I was the one who went into the worst neighborhood in the city to sell drugs every day, carrying a gun and talking bad. But I was scared too. I didn't know what to do.

"I don't think I'm going to make it, Michael. I think I'm going to die here."

"You can't! No! No! No! You can't leave me! You get home right now! Do you hear me? You get your ass home!"

I shook my head, still sobbing. I could barely hear Michael's voice over the screams and gunshots.

"I can't, Michael. I love you. I love you so much. But I can't make it."

"Bullshit!" Melody snatched the phone from my hands.

"Is this Michael?"

"Who is this?"

"This Melody. And Brandon is my friend, and I'm gonna get him home to you, you hear? He's gonna be all right. I'm gonna get him home. Now tell him you love him too so we can get out of here."

She handed me back the phone, and I just stood there with my jaw hanging open.

"Come home to me, Brandon. I love you. You do what that woman says. You come home to me."

But Michael didn't know that this crazy woman had been about to murder me with a kitchen knife two minutes ago.

"Let's go," Melody said, and grabbed me by the arm, pulling me down the alley, away from the bloodshed and slaughter taking place on the avenue. She still wore only a bathrobe, slippers, and was still carrying that same knife. She hadn't bothered picking up the revolver the guy she'd murdered had been carrying, content with her bloody kitchen utensil. I had to admit, it had served her well so far. Why change what works?

We walked three blocks until we came to a grocery store.

It was on fire. People were still looting the place even as it burned. The smell of burning flesh was unmistakable. There were people dying inside. The parking lot was full of cars, but not people. There were maybe a couple dozen people running out of the store with whatever they could carry that wasn't already incinerating. There must have been fifty cars in the parking lot though. Most of the people must have still been inside.

"You know how to hot-wire a car?" Melody asked.

"No."

"I do," Melody said. I wondered why she had bothered to ask me at all.

Melody walked over to an oversized SUV that looked like it got about a mile a gallon. She began hammering on the driver's side window with her fists, attempting to break through the glass. I looked around, scouring the parking lot for something to smash the window with. I found a hunk of concrete that had crumbled off one of the parking barricades. I picked it up and walked back over to Melody. I considered moving her aside and bashing the window myself, but Melody had become rather invested in breaking through that damn plexiglass, so invested she'd already beaten her hands bloody on it.

"Here," I said. "Try this." I handed her the hunk of concrete. A wicked smile tore across her face as she hefted the hunk of concrete in her hands. I knew what she was thinking. She could have easily cracked open my skull with it. Instead, she turned and smashed the window.

"Come on!" She reached through and unlocked the door, then dropped down and reached underneath the dashboard, ripping out wires. I hoped she knew what she was doing because it looked to me like all she was doing was damage. I saw her twist a few wires together, and suddenly, the big SUV engine roared to life.

"Fuck yeah!" She whooped, leaping into the air with childlike exuberance, and then her head exploded. I watched her skull rupture like a cantaloupe that had sat in the sun too long. Her gray matter and skull fragments splattered all over me. I ducked and looked around but couldn't see anyone shooting at us. There was so much shooting going on, it was hard to tell, though. But it seemed to have just been a stray bullet. Just bad luck.

"I'm sorry, Melody," I said, looking down at the empty, shattered shell that had housed that beautiful, mad woman as it leaked blood and brains onto the asphalt. "Thank you for helping me get home."

I heard a siren go off as I climbed behind the wheel of the SUV. I remembered hearing that same siren the previous day, right before the US announced the end of the war in the Middle East. They had "won" by killing every man, woman, and child in Iraq and Afghanistan. I thought the siren was some sort of celebration. Then I heard it again earlier in the day, when I was on the freeway, driving down here to meet with Dicky. It sounded like an old air raid siren, but louder, coming from all directions, blotting out every other noise. When it stopped, I was already driving out of the parking lot, heading down Washington Lane, taking my ass out of this crazy neighborhood, heading toward whatever madness awaited me in my own crazy neighborhood.

The radio was on. I hadn't been able to hear it over the siren, but it was finally dying down. It was a news station. NPR, I think. They were talking about all the drug violence that had taken hold of the city.

"Reports are coming in that this is not just a local phenomenon but a global one. The street drug called 'horse,' so called because of its red color and it's penchant for driving men to acts of violence, like the red horse of the apocalypse, has now spread across the globe. In cities across the world, rioting, assaults, murder, and looting has taken hold. Martial law has been declared in ..."

I zoned out, stuck on three words, "across the globe." It was everywhere. There was nowhere safe. Nowhere for us to go. I turned onto the freeway on-ramp, right into bumper-to-bumper traffic. But it wasn't just traffic. It was mayhem. It was a slaughterhouse. On the freeway, as far as the eye could see, people were being dragged from their cars, shot, stabbed, beaten, strangled, raped. Bodies littered the road beside and between stalled vehicles, making them impossible to pass. I pulled out my cellphone and began dialing Michael again. I had to tell him the bad news.

Chapter Fourteen

THE DEVIL IN THE RIVER

The Devil In The River

The devil's in the river
Grandpa said
as we sat on the banks
of boathouse row
swarmed by ducks and geese
quacking for food
As the sun dipped its toes
where the Schuylkill
met the horizon
But, I wanted to swim

I wanted relief
from that humid August
the oily stagnant Philly heat
hot and wet
with violence and frustration
sultry sweltering sex
I was too young to understand
but could feel all around me

a funky sweaty unctuousness
radiating from concrete and asphalt
full of pheromones
dripping from everything
the uncomfortable irritable anger
of air that doesn't move
that bakes on the concrete
like chicken grease

I wanted to swim

I wanted relief
from the kids who bullied me at school
from the kids who bullied me
in my neighborhood
from the pity in the eyes of adults

I wanted to swim

The Schuylkill River
dark coffee waters
Muddy and polluted
the blood of Filthydelphia
The City That Never Sweeps
The City of Bodily Harm
A pulsing artery of waste and rot
Only a child
a ghetto child
who'd never seen the sea
would want to swim
in that murky effluence
that river of filth

Only a ghetto child
who'd never gone fishing
never hung his feet off a pier

never hung his feet
over the side of a boat
never had a backyard pool
with a diving board
for belly flops and cannonballs
would want to dive
in that dank opaque stew
of garbage
thick slimy vegetation
and blind-wriggling life

The devil's in the river
Grandpa said

The devil was in the basement
The devil was in the attic
In the alleyways at night
In the park
after the streetlights came on
Grandma's wine closet
Grandpa's medicine drawer
The devil was everywhere
Grandpa didn't want me to go

Only a ghetto child
who'd never had a real father
raised by his grandfather
with superstition and fear
would go back to the river
as a teenager
as an orphan
still wanting to swim
in that polluted soup

The devil's in the river
Grandpa said

But Grandpa was gone now
Buried next to Grandma
And great Grandpa
And great Grandma
And great great uncles and aunts
And Mom

The Devil didn't get him
High blood pressure did
And emphysema
And Salem light 100s
And M/D 2020
And 40 hard back-breaking years
as a brick Mason
And 80 years of fried greasy food
And 80 years without proper health care
But not the devil
Not the river

I watched
the brown-capped waves
rowing teams sluicing through them
kids with their parents
feeding the hungry ducks and geese
quacking for crumbs of bread
widowed old men and women
sitting on benches
staring into the brown water
wondering if their loved ones
were down there with the devil
I wondered if Grandpa
or Grandma
or Mom
was down there
in that brown stew
with the devil

They were all bad
all sinners
I had seen them sin
heard them sin
felt them sin
If the devil was in there
down there
so were they

I wondered
what arcane incantation
would bring the devil forth
bring mom
and grandma
and grandpa
out of the Schuylkill
Then
I saw it

Slithering
serpentine
undulations
A dark adder
A massive shadow
sliding through the murk

I remember
watching the otters at the zoo
Aquatic acrobats
Gliding and sliding through the water
The shadow moved like that
But bigger
Much much bigger
The size of a submarine
As big as the biggest whale
With eyes and teeth

Tusks like an angler fish
But bigger
Much much bigger

I watched it break the water
that dank, muddy, brown water
watched it glide slowly toward the shore
Blue white eyes
orbs of electric fire
bioluminescent balls of lightning
as large as my head
fixed on prey

Downstream
A man sat fishing
A homeless man
In a dirty brown jacket
wearing dirty brown jeans
that may have been blue once
I wanted to warn him
I wanted to scream for him to flee
I knew what was coming
I watched what was coming
Silently

Those eyes
Those teeth
Tusks like an angler fish
But bigger
Much much bigger
I watched that maw slowly open
Wider
Wider
Wider
Wide enough to swallow a Buick
Wide enough to swallow the man

with the dirty brown jacket
the dirty brown jeans
that may have been blue once

I heard the startled scream
the too-late-to-escape
too late to fight
too late to pray
scream
screams
Saw teeth pierce flesh
that serpentine body
thrash like a shark
like a dog with a chew toy
watched it roll like an alligator
as it dragged the man under
I saw the devil
drag the man under
the Schuylkill River
drag him to hell
with Grandpa
and Grandma
and Mom

I never screamed
or shouted a warning
I just watched as
the devil took the man
in the dirty brown jacket
and dirty brown jeans
that may have been blue once

I looked around
at the rowing teams
sluicing through the brown-capped waves
the kids with their parents

feeding the hungry ducks and geese
quacking for crumbs of bread
widowed old men and women
sitting on benches
staring into the brown water
wondering if their loved ones
were down there with the devil
Like I wondered if Grandpa
was down there
in that brown stew
with the devil
Like I wondered
if Grandma
and great Grandpa
and great Grandma
and my great great uncles and aunts
and Mom
were down there
in that brown stew
with the devil
and I wondered if I had imagined it
and what that meant

I watched
as night slithered in
merged with the dark river
with the dark thing inside the river
and I thought
about the kids at school
about the bullies at school
about the kids in my neighborhood
about the bullies in my neighborhood
and I wondered
how to get them
to come fishing with me
on boathouse row

at sunset
at twilight
I wondered
if the devil would come out again
and drag them down
into that dank, murky, brown
river of effluence
drag them to hell
with grandpa.

I heard once
predators were attracted to blood
like sharks and alligators
I heard once
demons and devils
were conjured with blood
the blood of the innocent
virgin blood
Maybe
the devil would come
if I cut them first
an offering of blood
a sacrifice
I will cut them first
to conjure the devil
call it forth from the brown river
to drag them to hell
where those little bastards belong.

Chapter Fifteen

SCREAMS IN BOBBY'S EYES

Years before we saw the body
disemboweled
dismembered
disconnected
from the boy we'd all known
the happy
goofy
cocky
asshole
we'd all known
we already knew
Bobby was a murderer

His eyes were full of shrill screams
that were not his own
Since the second grade
Since that day we all first met

Sammy
Rick
Tyrone

Trisha
Latonya
Bobby
and me

We met on the playground swings
On a day so hot
the sun blazed off the sidewalk
A blistering white
like we were walking on sunlight

Shimmering waves of June heat
rose from the metal slide
And there sat Bobby
with a magnifying glass
immolating ants

Sammy threw a ball to Rick
Tyrone threw a frisbee
to Latonya and Trisha
And I sat watching Bobby
Murdering ants in dozens

He'd always been sadistic
We knew
We knew
Since he showed us the dead birds
All of those dead birds
Burned
Stabbed
Strangled
Impaled
Bludgeoned
And dismembered
disemboweled
disconnected from the skies

With tools from his dad's toolbox

Just like that Prince song
Bobby made the doves cry
And scream
And bleed

Bobby's father left long ago
Left him with a scar
Like a river on a map
That wound down his forehead

He left him with many wounds
So many wounds
And painful memories
And terrors
And tears
And screams
And desires
And a toolbox
Full of tools
He never taught Bobby to use
But Bobby was creative
So very
very
creative

He couldn't fix his bike chain
Or replace the tire
when the wheels went flat
Or put the limbs back
on his sister's broken dolls
Or repair the computer
where his dad kept the photos
The ones Bobby told us about
After he showed us the birds

The ones of all those children
who looked like Bobby
who died just like those birds
in Bobby's secret treehouse

There were so many feathers
Feathers everywhere
Plastered to the floor
Drifting in the air
Sticking to the walls
White
Gray
Brown
wet
red
feathers
And severed wings
like an abattoir
of slaughtered angels

Bobby told us all about
those bloody photos
on his father's computer
Pointed to each bird
carefully posed
just like the photos
And described each child
with a smile on his face
but not in his eyes
but not in his voice
Chilly as an autumn wind

We already knew
Bobby was a murderer
But he was our friend

The other kids at our school
were all afraid of Bobby
The other kids at our school
should be afraid of Bobby

Bobby was our attack dog
He kept us all safe
safe from all the bullies
He would whisper in their ears
Tell them about his toolbox
Tell them about the birds
And he would smile
But not his eyes
Eyes full of shrill screams
that were not his own
Eyes full of shrill screams
that might be theirs
if they persisted

When Trisha's father hurt her
her wicked stepdad
who did wicked things to her
hurt her in the night
when her mother was asleep

She came to Bobby and us
She came to Bobby
because she knew
she knew
we knew
what Bobby would do

When her stepdad disappeared
we all smiled
with our eyes
full of shrill screams

that were not our own
We knew what Bobby had done
We knew what we had all done
Even if we didn't "know"
We knew
We knew

What we didn't know back then
What we would all learn later
Was that this was Bobby's first
Trisha's stepfather
Bobby's first without feathers
First that screamed words
That begged for his life
That made Bobby feel something

We made him a murderer
We made him our murderer
And
Bobby
Could
Not
Stop
Bobby never stopped

When we all began high school
When we all drifted apart
We still thought about Bobby
When kids
Or parents
Or teachers
went missing
We all thought about Bobby

When Sammy became a jock
became a bully

became an asshole
began to harass us
began to terrorize us
we all thought about Bobby
Everyone except Sammy

Sammy must have forgotten
the blood and feathers
the slaughtered angels
Trisha's stepfather
the eyes that never smiled
Eyes full of shrill screams
that were not his own

Sammy must have forgotten
Sammy must have forgotten

Sammy must have remembered
When the hammer struck his hands
When the hammer struck his shins
When the hammer struck his knees
When the hammer struck his elbows
When the white of splintered bone
erupted through red meat
and yellow fat
and tanned skin

When his shrill screams
filled Bobby's ears

Sammy must have remembered
When the screwdriver pierced his hands
When the screwdriver pierced his feet
When the screwdriver pierced his testicles
When the screwdriver pierced his eardrums
When the screwdriver pierced his eyeballs

Sammy must have remembered
When the saw cut off his hands
When the saw cut off his feet

Cut off his calves
Cut of his biceps
Cut off his pectorals
his buttocks
his cock
his head

When his silence
filled Bobby's eyes
When his silence echoed
like a whisper in a tomb
through Bobby's treehouse

It was the first time in years
that we were all together
in Bobby's treehouse

Sammy
Rick
Tyrone
Trisha
Latonya
Bobby
and me

Except Sammy wasn't together
Sammy was everywhere
His skin
His bones
His organs
His muscles
His popcorn-colored fat

was everywhere
plastered to the walls
sticking to the floor
like an abattoir
of slaughtered teenagers
slaughtered classmates
slaughtered assholes
who used to be our friend

Years before
we saw Sammy's body
we already knew
Bobby was a murderer
But Bobby was our friend
But Bobby killed our friend
For us
For himself
For his father

Years before
we saw Sammy's body
we saw all those bodies
pieces of pieces
of pieces of bodies
we already knew
that Bobby had to die

Bobby smiled at us
but not his eyes
His eyes were full of shrill screams
that were not his own

We smiled back at him
But not our eyes
We already knew
that Bobby had to die

We each removed a tool
from Bobby's father's toolbox
Rick took a hacksaw
Tyrone a claw hammer
Trisha found a keyhole saw
Latonya a pry bar
And I picked up a mallet
And Bobby took it all

And our eyes all filled
with Bobby's shrill screams.

Chapter Sixteen

EATING WITH MOMMA

Something inside
was killing us
Momma told me

I had to feed it
We had to feed it
or it would eat me
from the marrow
to the bone
to the muscles and sinew
through my skin
like maggots on carrion
and feed itself
on those nearest to me

It was in all of us
Momma said
Only us
A family thing

We were the last

Momma said
The last who once hunted
beneath a sky of infinite stars
unpolluted by electricity
through stygian forests
beneath the canopy
of centuries-old trees
on nights so dark
only scent and sound would guide us

The last
Momma said
who ran
beneath a round
white-faced
crater-pocked moon
grass beneath our paws
blood on our lips
meat between our teeth
Who were hunted
to extinction

We had to survive
Momma said
I had to survive
Momma said
We were the last

This thing inside us
That was us
That made us
something terrible
Something ravenous
Something vicious
remorseless
relentless

voracious
eating away at me
An infection
A virus of the flesh
the mind
the soul
A parasite
Dark and ancient
Primal and terrible

I tried to starve it
Starve it to death
Momma said it would eat me
If I didn't feed it
I could feel it
Tearing at my insides
Like a belly full of piranha

I imagined
feeding someone
to those piranha in my belly
The boy
who delivered the morning paper
The old man
in the ripped and stained blue jeans
with patches on his knees
who went fishing at the lake
Saturday mornings
catching nothing but memories
The girl
in the yellow sundress
and black and white Chuck Taylors
who skateboarded past my house
on a bright and breezy
quiet Sunday morning

I imagined her screaming
I imagined eating
her bubbly yellow fat
her stringy red
fibrous muscle
her plump juicy organ meat
cracking open bone
sucking out the marrow

I imagined her screaming
I imagined the hunger gone
the pain gone
the peace
Momma said I would feel
Something inside me growled
Something ravenous
Something vicious
remorseless
relentless
voracious
eating away at me
An infection
A virus of the flesh
the mind
the soul
A parasite
Dark and ancient
Primal and terrible

I could feel it
In my mind
in the twilight spaces
between my thoughts
whispering evil things
terrible things
wet delicious things

like Lucifer in the desert
like the serpent in the garden
like the Son of Sam's
neighbor's dog
demanding murder
Seducing me
with wet
delicious
terrible
things

Momma brought me meat
red
dripping
screaming
begging
meat

"Eat child."

I couldn't
I wouldn't
The meat
was the same age as me
Had terrified eyes
Terrified screams
Terrified words

"Please, help me!"

"Eat child, or you'll die,"
Momma said

I couldn't
I wouldn't
The meat

had parents
It told me
had a little sister
younger than mine
It told me
had dreams
It told me
Wanted to be a dancer
A surfer
A nurse
A skateboard champion
A race car driver
Not meat
Not food
It told me

The meat
wore a yellow sundress
and black and white Chuck Taylors

"Please don't!"

"Eat child"

I shook my head
I couldn't
I wouldn't
Momma did
Sister did

Momma tore out it's throat
Quick as a viper
I watched her chew
and swallow
chew
and swallow

chew
and swallow
My stomach growled
That thing inside me
growled

"Eat child," Momma said again.
"Eat or you'll die."

Momma ate
My little sister ate
I wanted to
That deep
dark
terrible
primal thing
inside
wanted to eat
But the meat was staring at me
So scared
So alone
Bleeding
Dying
Suffering
Alone
I held its hand
Told it to go to sleep
It would be over soon
While Momma bit
and tore
and thrashed
and chewed
and swallowed
and that yellow sundress
turned red
and I was so hungry

"Momma only wants what's best for you.
Momma only wants to see you grow strong
Momma wants you to survive."

Momma wants me to kill
Momma wants me to be like her
Momma wants the monster inside me
the infection
the virus
the parasite
to live
inside me

Tomorrow
she would bring
more meat
The boy
who delivered the Sunday paper
The old man
in the ripped and stained blue jeans
with patches on his knees
who went fishing at the lake
Saturday mornings

Or maybe a baby
a newborn
with the scent of baby powder
and diaper cream
like last time

Or maybe a teenager
with tattoos and piercings
reeking of sweat
and cigarettes
beer
and marijuana

and fear

Momma would bring more meat
Tomorrow
And the next day
And the next
Until this thing inside me
Ate

"Why? Why do I have to be like this?"

"It's who we are. It's what we are."

I didn't want to be like Momma
I didn't want to be this thing
that ate pretty girls
in yellow sundresses
and black and white Chuck Taylors

"You have to eat."

So I did
That night
I ate

I ate my fingers
chewing each digit
to the bone
sucking out the marrow

I ate my hands
ripping at the palms
through callouses
into the chewy stringy red meat
my arms
up to the elbows

my neck and back
stretched and contorted impossibly
to reach
further and further

I chewed
and swallowed
chewed
and swallowed
chewed
and swallowed
and tore
and thrashed
and screamed
and cried

My stomach growled
That thing inside me
growled
and I ate
and ate
and ate
bending and contorting
like a serpent
to reach more
to eat more
bubbly yellow fat
stringy red
fibrous muscle
plump juicy organ meat
until this thing inside me
was quiet
satiated
the hunger gone
the pain gone

Momma said
I had to feed it
We had to feed it
this thing inside me
This ravenous
vicious
remorseless
relentless
voracious
thing
eating away at me
or it would eat me
from the marrow
to the bone
to the muscles and sinew
through my skin
like maggots on carrion
and feed itself
on those nearest to me
But now
I
would feed those nearest to me
I
would feed Momma
I
would feed sister
I
would feed
the thing in all of us
the hunger gone
the pain gone
the peace
the peace.

Chapter Seventeen

BIG BROTHER

Jamal turned up the volume on his headphones to drown out the agonized shrieks and cries. He frowned, brow furrowed in annoyance. He didn't mind all the squirming and jerking around. The man wasn't going anywhere anyway, but all that racket was close to ruining the moment.

The man screamed like a slapped infant. Begged and cried. Shouted curses, promises, safe words they'd never negotiated, anything to get Jamal to stop fucking him. Veins and chords bulged prominently in his neck and forehead like they were seconds from popping free of his skin and spraying the room like wiggling water tubes at a children's splash park.

An artery pulsed in his temple. Sweat poured from his brow and rained down his face as he cried out in agony again and again, struggling to endure the unbearable strain of this intimate invasion. But, in Jamal's world, consent could not be withdrawn. He'd made that clear before they began.

"Once I'm inside you, I ain't pulling out until I cum."

"I wouldn't want you to, Daddy," the clueless man replied. How deep his regret for that statement ran was now etched into every sweat-filled crevice in that rictus of agony grimacing and shrieking as Jamal thrust up into his guts.

Tears, snot, and long ropes of saliva drooled off the man's chin forming a small pink puddle on the black latex-covered mattress. Jamal mentally patted himself on the back for having the foresight to put latex sheets on the bed instead of the bamboo or Egyptian cotton he preferred. Replacing sheets was expensive, unless you bought the cheap shit, and Jamal had enough trouble sleeping without rough scratchy sheets. Tears and snot were far from the worst thing he would be cleaning from those sheets by the end of the evening. He hoped he'd at least be spared the inconvenience of disposing of a corpse.

The screaming reached a pitch that was almost earsplitting. Jamal's earphones fell out as he increased his thrusts, racing toward orgasm. He fumbled them loosely back into place, then gave up on them entirely when they fell out again. They were a good idea. Jamal just needed to refine the execution. He'd even put together a collection of songs he thought would help get and keep him in the mood, an eclectic combination of R&B, hip-hop, and heavy metal power ballads. It usually did the trick. He just needed to find earphones that fit his ears better and didn't fall out at critical moments.

Jamal had gotten used to the screaming. He'd tried his best to learn to love the sound, but he wasn't a sadist or a psychopath. Apathy was the best he could manage. At least all that begging and crying no longer killed his erection. He guessed that made him a bit of a sociopath. He'd heard psychopaths were born, but sociopaths were made by circumstances and environment. Jamal blamed his physical circumstances for his sexual violence. He had no choice. That's what he told himself repeatedly as he tried to block out the screams and concentrate on his orgasm, which remained just out of reach, but so very close.

The wet rhythmic splorsh of blood and possibly organs being displaced, reminded Jamal of plunging a toilet. He found the association appropriate though nonetheless unpleasant. The splash of blood and excrement accompanying each thrust was utterly nauseating. Very little about fucking Sam or Stephen or Sinclair, or whatever this dude's name was, in the ass was enjoyable on a purely sensual level except how it felt on his cock. That sensation was heaven itself. It was worth enduring the other brutal auditory and olfactory insults.

Men love to brag about the size of their dicks. It's a thing. Their sophomoric boasts are mostly outrageous lies and impossible exaggerations. A man with a cock barely five inches long will compare its length and girth to a firehose or a python. If he's lucky enough to be over six inches he'll tell everyone he's hung like a donkey, and brag about blowing backs out. And, if he's over eight inches, his lovers will gladly cosign that he's packing an anaconda in his pants. Men with small dicks, however, were a constant target for ridicule. There was no bigger insult than telling a guy he was underdeveloped in the penis area. Jamal hated all that bragging and bullshitting.

When he was a teenager, he'd happily participated in all of it. Then he began to wonder why it was okay to body-shame men with small dicks in a way that would be completely frowned upon if it were a woman with small tits or no ass. Everyone would think you were an asshole for body shaming a woman, but little dicked men were fair game, and guys with massive dicks were revered as much as women with huge breasts. It was all pretty ridiculous.

By the time he was thirteen Jamal already knew he was above average. He'd seen his father in the shower and was shocked to discover he was nearly twice as long as his dad. Then he kept growing.

His friends thought it was funny. One day, when they were all bragging about their dick sizes, comparing them to elephant trunks and horses, Jamal had enough of it.

"You wouldn't like it if you really did have a dick that big," Jamal said. Then, he showed them.

"Jesus Christ! Look at that fucking thing!"

"Oh, my god! It's almost as long as your leg!"

After that, rather than abating, the body shaming had increased. Only now, Jamal was the target. They told jokes about his oversized cock. They told him he should get into porn. Called him "Tripod" or "King Dong". They would ask him to whip it out and show their new friends. They would scare girls with tales of it. Then Jamal hit puberty and it grew again. It had never stopped growing. Jamal was almost thirty now.

When he began dating, even his friends soon realized it wasn't the gift they imagined it would be. Most women were horrified by it. They didn't want it anywhere near them. The majority of men were equally terrified of it, though often intrigued. And some, like the man Jamal was currently ripping in half, took it as a challenge. A challenge they most often failed, and failed gruesomely. Their screams of agony usually ended in a trip to the emergency room to repair a prolapsed anus, and bruised organs, or worse. Usually worse.

He'd met Stephen or Samuel or whatever his name was at a Leather bar in Houston. The man was getting anally fisted by a big leather bear with wrists and forearms thicker than Jamal's calves. The man doing the fisting had a ruler tattooed on his forearm. He said it was to show how deep he'd gotten his arm in a lover's asshole. He added another inch or two every time he was able to go deeper. The guy he was fisting that night was going to cause him to add at least another three inches to his tattoo. That ruler completely disappeared as the man's arm went up Samuel's ass to the elbow. Jamal was pretty sure the guy's name was Samuel. Maybe Steward?

Watching the scene gave Jamal hope. Maybe this guy could take him? He waited until the scene with the big bear was over before approaching the man with the nearly bottomless anus.

"That was impressive."

The guy looked Jamal up and down with a raised eyebrow and pursed lips.

"Thank you. You're pretty handsome, but I think your arms are too short and skinny for me."

Steward or Samuel or Stephen, let's just call him Steward for the sake of simplicity, waived a hand at Jamal dismissively. Jamal seized Steward's hand and guided it to his crotch. Jamal wore baggy jeans to hide his deformity, but its length and girth could be clearly felt through the thin layer of black denim.

"What the fuck? That's your cock?" He looked shocked, but not revolted or repulsed. That was good. Jamal nodded timidly.

"How big does that thing get when it's hard? I mean fully erect?"

Jamal smiled.

"Why don't you come home with me and find out?"

Jamal wasn't gay. At least, he didn't think he was. He was probably bisexual. He really didn't care what was attached to the hole he stuck his penis in. Man, woman, horse, cow, he couldn't give a fuck as long as it lasted long enough for him to cum. He did prefer vaginas, but he took whatever was available. A hole was a hole. It was all pink on the inside.

Jamal was an opportunist. His sexual preference was for sex as opposed to no sex, and most women weren't into guys who could jack up a car with their cocks. He'd had a few, and they honestly faired better than the men. Vaginas were designed to spit out eight-pound babies. They could take a pretty good pounding theoretically. But his dalliances with women never progressed beyond the occasional booty calls. It generally took less than a month before the calls stopped entirely, when the women tired of getting their insides bruised and organs rearranged and found men of more manageable endowment.

So, Jamal favored men for strictly utilitarian reasons. Mostly because their massive egos would not allow some of them to admit they weren't up to taking on the weapon of ass destruction Jamal called a penis. He'd even had one guy dislocate his jaw in his determination to prove he could fit Jamal's cock in his mouth. In his defense, once his jaw unhinged, Jamal's dick did kind of fit. Kind of.

Steward was one of those ego-driven types. Being able to fit fists and dildos the size of chair legs in his anus was sort of Steward's brand. Taking Jamal's cock would give him a whole new level of street cred. Jamal was excited about the possibility of a regular lover. He really didn't enjoy hunting for new ones every week. It was a necessary evil. So, when Steward wriggled out of his tight leather shorts and bent over to show a gaping anus wide enough to pitch a baseball through, Jamal was hopeful.

That hope was dashed after the first thrust into Steward's heavily lubed anus. Steward could just barely take Jamal's girth, a feat unto itself, but the length of Jamal's member was causing him problems. It only took three strokes for Steward to start screaming. Luckily, Steward had allowed himself to be tied up first. Face down. Ass up, with his forearms tied to his shins so he couldn't get out of that position to save his life.

Jamal was more aggressive with Steward than he had been with others. He supposed the man might have been okay if Jamal took it a little easier, shortened his strokes a little, went a little slower. But Jamal was fucking sick of taking it easy. He wanted to smash! And, Steward had agreed to it.

"I want you to fuck the shit out of me with that big ole dick of yours. I promise you I can take it. I have a dildo that's almost as big as you. It's about three feet long and sixteen inches around. I can almost get the whole thing inside. You fuck me as hard as you want big boy."

And so, Jamal did. He fucked Steward until blood flowed from his rectum like an open faucet. Jamal fucked him until each stroke sent blood and bile belching from Steward's mouth like projectile vomit. He fucked him until Steward stopped screaming and lay still. But most importantly, he fucked Steward until he had the most glorious soul-shattering orgasm, shouting his joy to the heavens as he erupted deep in Steward's pulverized bowels.

Jamal collapsed beside Steward's shallowly breathing body, landing in a puddle of blood and excrement. A shower was inevitable. It would just have to wait a little longer. Jamal began to feel drowsy as he listened to Steward's breathing slowly still and watched his pupils widen and fix in place. Jamal didn't particularly get off on killing people with his cock. Usually. The few times it happened it had been an accident. Except this time. This time he had to admit there was something exhilarating about every moment of it, including the last. He might have even begun to enjoy Steward's screams. But was it just Steward or could he get off like that with anyone if he just stopped giving a fuck and used them all like the fuck toys they were? Maybe it was trying not to kill them that was inhibiting Jamal's pleasure? He needed to try this again, and soon.

Recently, Jamal had been talking to a couple he'd met

online. They were your typical White couple looking for a Black "bull" with a "BBC" to fuck them both. Jamal found the whole thing so incredibly racist, but his choices were limited. When he was done with Steward, he decided he would arrange a meeting with the couple.

After a few brief conversations online, Jamal agreed to a phone call. He called them from a burner phone he often used in case things went badly. Things almost always went badly. Whatever was left of Jamal's conscience, any hesitation he may have felt at the idea of destroying this couple for his own sexual pleasure, ended with their first conversation.

"My husband is a cuckold. He likes watching me get fucked by big Black men. He thinks Black men are naturally superior lovers. They're so aggressive and animalistic. I just find Black men to be more dominant. They just take what they want."

Jamal rolled his eyes. Every sentence she spoke was one racist stereotype after another.

"Uh huh, and what else?"

"I consider myself a queen of spades. I've always been attracted to Black men and they've always been attracted to me. They love my big ass I guess. Did you see my photos?"

"Yes. That's why I responded to your message."

"Did you like what you saw?"

"That's why I responded."

"Black men love my big white ass."

"If you like Black dick so much, why did you marry a white guy?"

"Well, you know, my family, and that sort of thing just isn't done where I grew up."

"I see."

"Besides, I made sure I married a man who wouldn't mind me fucking other men. My husband loves big Black dick too.

He's into humiliation. It's his biggest kink. He loves it when I insult him while I'm getting fucked by a man with a bigger dick than his. He likes me to tell him how little and pathetic he is and how it takes a BBC to really please me. He's also bisexual, so he likes to be forced to lick another man's cum out of my pussy or even my asshole, for me to spit it in his mouth or for me to make him suck another man's cock and swallow the cum. And sometimes, I make him take it up the ass. He loves taking big Black dick in his ass."

What was most disturbing and disappointing about the entire conversation was that Jamal had heard it all before. Too many times. And the words were almost verbatim, as if they were all reading from the same script. He blamed porn. Porn was one of the last bastions of pure, unfiltered, shameless racism in American media.

They agreed to meet in a coffee shop. Jamal chose a round booth so they could all sit next to each other. Michael was thin and tall with a pleasant smile and skin that looked like it never saw the sun. Charlotte could have been his sister, except she was a big girl. Not quite a BBW, but she had thick hips and thighs, and cantaloupe-sized breasts just big enough to outstretch a belly that had birthed a couple children and never fully regained it's shape. Her ass was like two beach balls pressed together. He knew her story just by looking at her. With an ass like that she'd probably been chased by black men since high school.

"So, what's up with your obsession with Black men?" Michael asked, addressing Michael.

Michael shrugged, and looked sheepish.

"I just think Black men are sexier. I like the way your muscles look beneath your dark skin. I like how dark skin looks against white skin. The contrast is beautiful. Seeing Charlotte's mouth around a big black cock is hot as fuck. And, I grew up listening to hip-hop, and gangster rap. I know all

Black people aren't gangsters and thugs, but when I first realized I was bi, it was black gangsters I used to fantasize about fucking me. I mean, I know not all Black men are hung like horses, but that's the myth right? When you watch porn, interracial porn, all the black guys have nine and ten-inch cocks, so that kinda became my fantasy."

"It's almost exactly the same for me. Plus, I'm a thicker girl," Charlotte said. "And Black guys always seemed to appreciate my curves more. They don't make me feel fat. I feel sexy when I'm with a black guy. And I love it when they cum inside of me. I like the fantasy of being impregnated by a Black man. It's such a taboo where I grew up. I would be the scandal of the town and probably disowned by my family. And, I love watching Michael lick Black cum out of me or off of me. I like seeing him humiliated like that."

"It's just cum."

"What?"

"It isn't 'Black cum' or 'White cum' or 'Asian or Hispanic cum'. It's just cum. It's all the same."

"Oh, you know what I mean."

Jamal nodded.

"Uh huh."

It was a decent enough explanation, honest, sincere, and racist as fuck. The fetishization and objectification of Black men was almost as bad as what Asian women endured, or so Jamal imagined. I mean, he wouldn't know, but he could guess. Even the term "BBC" was rooted in the dehumanization of Black men, reducing them to their sex organs. Admitting they were aware their preferences were based on racist stereotypes was somehow both better and worse. It was time to discuss the elephant trunk in the room.

"Before we go much further, I think I need to show you something."

Charlotte and Michael looked at each other.

"Show us what?"

Jamal became very serious. He was wearing his usual baggy oversized jeans.

"Give me your hands."

He looked like some kind of spiritual guru as he held out his hands, palms up, for Charlotte and Michael to take. They each slid a palm in his and he guided them down between his legs.

"Oh my God! Is that real? That can't be real."

"Get the fuck out of here! How can that be real? You're fucking with us," Michael laughed. Charlotte started laughing too. Jamal remained stoic.

"You're crazy. What's that, some kind of a strap-on?"

Jamal locked eyes with Michael.

"Come to the men's room with me."

His seriousness silenced their laughter. Charlotte and Michael looked at each other then looked back at Jamal whose face was a mask of stone.

"You're serious? There's no way."

"Come find out."

Jamal stood up and began walking toward the men's room. Michael rose also, confusion and a hint of fear battled with his curiosity as he looked at his wife once again before following Jamal. She looked worried, but excited.

Michael followed Jamal toward the back of the coffee shop and through a door marked with a shirtless cartoon bull wearing tight blue jeans with bulging biceps and pectoral muscles, across the hall from an identical door marked with a sexy cartoon cow in a halter top and mini skirt. Jamal held the door open for Michael who kept looking back at his wife as if he was afraid he was about to be mugged or raped.

"It's okay. I won't bite. I just want you to know what you are getting into."

The bathroom had a single toilet, one sink, and a single urinal. The door handle had a lock that Jamal engaged as soon as Micheal stepped in behind him.

"Okay. You ready?"

"Yeah. Ummm. Okay. I'm ready. I guess. There's no way you're going to make me believe that's a real cock."

Jamal unbuckled his pants and let his size 42 jeans slip from his 32" hips to the floor. Michael let out a gasp and his hands flew to his face. He took a few steps back like he expected the thing to attack him.

"Oh shit! What the fuck?!"

He looked horrified. Jamal did his best to control his anger, but he was strongly considering force-feeding his cock down Michael's throat. Slowly, the horror on Micheal's face morphed into something more akin to awe and wonder.

"Can I ... can I touch it?"

Jamal nodded. "Be my guest."

Michael knelt down, bowing on one knee to reach the head of Jamal's cock, cradling the entire thing in his arms like a newborn baby.

"It's magnificent. But ... but how did this happen? Did you get some kind of surgery? Grow up next to a nuclear power plant?"

Jamal frowned.

"Rule number one. No jokes. It's a sensitive subject for me."

"Okay. My bad. I'm sorry. It's just – this is a lot to take in, and I mean that literally!"

Jamal's frown deepened. His head dropped and shoulders slumped.

"So, then it's a no for you? You want to call this whole thing off?"

Micheal shrugged. He was still on his knees, holding Jamal's cock. He hadn't taken his eyes off of it.

"I don't know. I'll have to see what Charlotte says. If she wants to try it, I'm okay with it. I mean pussies can stretch, right? Babies come out of them, right?"

"Right. And so can assholes." Jamal said. "But she should have all the information before she makes a decision. You need to get it hard."

***

Michael walked out of the men's room shadowed by Jamal. He looked like he'd had a glimpse into hell.

"Michael, what's wrong?"

Michael shook his head.

"It's real," he whispered in a hoarse voice, then sat down at the table with his eyes wide, staring off into the distance. His mouth hung open as he rubbed his hands down his face from his forehead to his chin. Jamal and Charlotte both allowed him a moment to compose himself. Gradually Michael's gaze drifted toward Charlotte. He shook his head vigorously.

"It's too much," he said.

"What's too much? His cock?"

"Yes. I don't think you should. I don't think you can!"

Charlotte's eyes narrowed. Her mouth fell into a hard line on her face.

"You've seen what I can do, how much I can take."

Micheal shook his head again.

"Nothing like this. You didn't see it."

Jamal was beginning to get annoyed. He considered standing up and walking out on both of them, but a larger part of him wanted to punish them both for every dehumanizing thought they'd ever had about Black men. Another part really needed the cathartic release of an orgasm or two or three, and thought fucking both of these racist freaks to death would be amazing. Epic. And, it wouldn't leave even a small stain on his conscience. Besides, he really did like Charlotte's huge ass.

"It can't be that bad."

"You didn't see it."

Charlotte listened as Micheal described what he'd seen in the men's room. He was not expecting the look of undisguised feral lust that crossed her face. Neither was Jamal.

"I want him to fuck me."

"But, Charlotte –"

"And, I want you to watch... and maybe more."

"Yes, ma'am," Micheal said. He looked crestfallen.

"Oh, come on! This is going to be so much fun! You'll see. Stop looking like you're going to a funeral, for Christ's sake. Your woman is about to take on the biggest Black dick on the planet. You should be excited!"

"Crazy bitch," Jamal thought.

They did a brief negotiation. Jamal insisted, as usual, that there would be no retracting consent.

"I want to make it clear that I will finish. Once we start fucking I won't stop until I bust a nut."

Charlotte smiled.

"Okay. I'm good with that. Are you good with that, Michael?"

"But, what if it's too much for you?"

"I said, are you good with that?"

Michael's shoulders slumped. He looked stricken, but nodded his acquiescence to her will. It was clear who the alpha in the relationship was.

"So, when?"

"How about tonight?"

Charlotte smiled.

"I can't wait."

***

Charlotte had the wettest pussy Jamal had ever felt. He supposed he should have been flattered that she was so turned on.

"Fuck me! Fuck me hard!"

She was dripping all down her thighs by the time he eased the tip in. Michael sat by the bedside, stroking his own modest erection. He wasn't a small man, just the average five and a half inches or so. Nothing to brag about, but nothing to laugh at either. Most women would have been happy with it. Micheal had just made the mistake of marrying the type of woman who needed her guts rearranged in order to feel satisfied.

"Come here!"

Jamal withdrew his cock and grabbed Micheal by the back of the head, forcing him to lick his wife's juices from the head of Jamal's dick. Michael was clearly aroused but just as clearly terrified.

"I want you to fuck him," Charlotte said. "Fuck him in his ass with that big black dick of yours."

Michael's eyes widened and he shook his head.

"There's no way. That would kill me."

"But this is what you've always fantasized about. It's what we have always fantasized about. All those nights when I was fucking you with my strap-on, we would talk about how we wished it was a huge black cock inside you. How I wanted to watch you get used by a superior Black man, a big bull with a cock as long and thick as my arm."

"But those were just fantasies. I never imagined anything that big."

Charlotte's eyes flashed brilliantly with rage.

"It wasn't just a fantasy to me! I want this! Are you saying no to your mistress?"

"No – I mean yes – I mean no, I'm not saying no."

"Then bend over and take that big nigger dick in your ass!"

And there it was. Jamal knew that word had been bubbling there under the surface, and now it emerged in all its racist glory.

Jamal turned and walked slowly back toward the bed, his penis swayed between his legs erect, but too large to resist the pull of gravity. He paused at the edge of the bed and seized Charlotte by the ankles, jerking her legs into the air and spreading them wide. She gasped, but looked excited. Not afraid.

"No, I think I want to fuck you first. Like I said, I finish what I start, and I already had the tip in. Let's give you all of this big nigger dick."

Inch by inch of his cock slid inside that luxuriously wet pussy. Charlotte grunted and grit her teeth, gasping and letting out the occasional shout as she struggled to take him all in.

"Be careful, Charlotte," Micheal said.

Jamal felt the sensation of a tongue encircling his cock. It was an amazing feeling. He closed his eyes and let himself enjoy it, as he slid in deeper and heard Charlotte cry out in pain, then he felt something bite his cock.

"Ouch! What the fuck was that?"

He felt it again, harder this time. He tried to withdraw, but something held his cock in place, clamping down harder and harder like it was trying to bite his dick in half.

"Ow! Fuck! What is that? What the fuck is inside of you?"

Charlotte's face was contorted in a familiar rictus of pain and effort as she attempted to take him all in, but there was something else there too, something sinister and oddly triumphant.

"Vagina dentata. I'm going to bite that big black cock right off!"

Jamal had never taken Latin, but it wasn't hard to figure out. The bitch's vagina had teeth!

"The fuck you are!"

Jamal punched her right in the face as hard as he could. Her nose bled and her eyes rolled back in her head. She was dazed for a moment, but still conscious. He tried to pull out again. Nothing. If anything, her pussy bit down even harder. He punched her again and again, bloodying her mouth and swelling her eye. Still, his dick remained stuck inside her.

"Hey! Stop hitting her!"

Michael charged at him from the side and Jamal had to

turn slightly to swing an awkward left hook that caught Michael flush on the chin. Luckily, Michael had a glass jaw. He dropped like a sack of meat. Jamal was still stuck, and now Charlotte's pussy wasn't just biting down, it was chewing.

Jamal tried again to pull his dick free of Charlotte's ravenous vagina, but she held on like a Pitbull on a sirloin steak. So, he did the next best thing. He thrusted forward as hard and fast as he could. Whatever her pussy was, it was designed to accept cock. Once you were inside it wouldn't let you out, but it would take all the dick you gave it, so Jamal gave it all. He thrusted balls deep into Charlotte, deeper than he'd ever entered anyone in his life. An explosion of gore belched from Charlotte's mouth and splattered Jamal's face. The tip of his cock parted her lips, coated in blood and entrails. He had impaled her with his cock, skewered right through her. Her lifeless body hung from his cock like a meat condom. The biting sensation was gone now.

"I told you, once I start, I'm finishing," Jamal said, as he began fucking the lifeless bleeding husk that had been Charlotte. Pumping her corpse like a piston. Blood and viscera exploded from her mouth with each brutal thrust. Her stomach and what looked like a full set of lungs were pushed out of her mouth on the head of Jamal's dick. If she wasn't dead before, she was good and dead now. Thick, dark, meaty red blood poured from her nose and ears like a cherry slushie machine. When Jamal finally came, the orgasm felt like it lasted an entire minute. He filled her vandalized corpse with nearly a gallon of his seed. His semen sprayed from her mouth and dripped from her nose.

Jamal slowly withdrew his diminishing blood-drenched erection from Charlotte's stretched, torn, and battered vagina. There were teeth marks on his dick. Her vagina teeth had broken the skin. Jamal couldn't tell how much of the blood was his and how much was Charlotte's. Some of the bite marks were pretty deep. She, or her pussy, had tried their best to bite it clean off. Only his enormous size had saved him. For once, the monstrous appendage swinging between his legs had been a blessing.

He looked down between Charlotte's legs, blood and semen leaked out of her in a slow but steady stream. A tongue lolled out of that gaping maw. Her vagina was lined with a full set of teeth that looked vaguely canine, four fangs, two on each side, followed by a couple dozen little sharp curved teeth like a Venus flytrap. It gave a whole new definition to man-eater.

"Oh my God! Charlotte! Charlotte!"

Jamal had almost forgotten about Michael. He turned and grabbed the little man by the back of the neck.

"Wasn't your job supposed to be clean up? Well, go ahead. Lick it up! Lick up every fucking drop!"

Jamal forced Micheal's face down between Charlotte's legs and into that ruined, bloody, cum-soaked snatch.

"Lick it up!"

He had to admit, he was a bit surprised when Michael began lapping at the blood and semen pooled in the folds of his dead wife's labia. Perhaps he wouldn't fuck Micheal to death after all, Jamal thought. Though the sound of Micheal's tongue licking Charlotte's pussy was getting him hard again.

FIRST APPEARANCES

"Unsolicited" first appeared in "Consumed: Tales Inspired by the Windigo", Denver Horror Collective, December 1, 2020

"Bloodsoaked Savior" first appeared in "Gorefest", Evil Cookie Publishing, August 22, 2021

"Horse" first appeared in "And Hell Followed", Death's Head Press, January 15, 2019

"The Screams In Bobby's Eyes" first appeared in "Bludgeon Tools: Splatterpunk Anthology, The Evil Cookie Publishing, January 1, 2021

"Blue & Red" first appeared in "The Dystopian States of America: A Charity Anthology Benefitting the ACLU", Haverhill House Publishing LLC, February 28, 2020

"Krokodile" first appeared in "Battered Broken Bodies: A Horror Anthology based on Body Horror", November 16, 2021

"Beast Mode" first appeared in "Masters of Horror: A Horror Anthology, Matt Shaw, November 5, 2017

"First Person Shooter" first appeared in Cemetery Dance issue #77, July 2019

ACKNOWLEDGMENTS

I would like to thank Shane Staley for publishing my early short stories in Delirium Webzine. Larry Roberts of Bloodletting Press for taking a chance on the insanity that was Succulent Prey and publishing my first novel. Don D'Auria for being crazy enough to accept Succulent Prey as a mass market paperback and stick it on bookshelves. Brian Keene for always believing in me and promoting my work like it was a second job. Edward Lee for collaborating with me on Teratologist when I was still relatively unknown. Monica J. O'Rourke for not only collaborating with me, but also editing so much of my work. Tod Clark for being a dedicated beta reader and proofreader. Thanks to all the women I've ever loved, made love to, or otherwise swapped fluids with. Every one of you contributed to my madness in some way, good or bad.

Special thanks to my little Cupcake, Patricia Mosier, who's love and service allowed me the time and energy as well as the motivation and inspiration to write this thing.

And, of course Leza Cantoral and Christoph Paul for working so hard to get this nasty piece of work into print.

ABOUT THE AUTHOR

WRATH JAMES WHITE is a former World Class Heavy-weight Kickboxer, a professional Kickboxing and Mixed Martial Arts trainer, distance runner, performance artist, and former street brawler, who is now known for creating some of the most disturbing works of fiction in print. Wrath is the author of such extreme horror classics as *The Resurrectionist* (now a major motion picture titled *Come Back To Me*) *Succulent Prey*, and its sequel *Prey Drive*, *400 Days of Oppression*, *If You Died Tomorrow I Would Eat Your Corpse*, and many others. He is the co-author of *Teratologist* co-written with the king of extreme horror, Edward Lee, *Something Terrible* co-written with his son Sultan Z. White, *Orgy of Souls* co-written with Maurice Broaddus, *Hero* and *The Killings* both co-written with J.F. Gonzalez, *Poisoning Eros* co-written with Monica J. O'Rourke, *Master of Pain* among others. Wrath lives and works in Austin, TX.

ALSO BY WRATH JAMES WHITE

Hardcore Kelli

Fight For Me

If You Died Tomorrow I Would Eat Your Corpse

400 Days of Oppression

Population Zero

His Pain

The Resurrectionist

Yaccub's Curse

Succulent Prey

The Book of A Thousand Sins

Like Porno For Psychos

Skinzz

ALSO BY CLASH BOOKS

WE PUT THE LIT IN LITERARY

CLASHBOOKS.COM

FOLLOW US

FB

TWITTER

IG

@clashbooks

EMAIL

clashmediabooks@gmail.com

CPSIA information can be obtained
at www.ICGtesting.com
Printed in the USA
JSHW081509110723
44567JS00001B/132